Landon Snow

and the Auctor's Kingdom

R. K. MORTENSON

BARBOUR
PUBLISHING

Landon Snow

and the Auctor's Kingdom

Cover and interior illustrations by Cory Godbey, Portland Studios.
www.portlandstudios.com

Cover design by Kirk DouPonce, DogEared Design, llc.

Published by Barbour Publishing, Inc., P.O. Box 719, Uhrichsville, OH 44683, www.barbourbooks.com

Our mission is to publish and distribute inspirational products offering exceptional value and biblical encouragement to the masses.

Member of the
Evangelical Christian
Publishers Association

Printed in the United States of America.

Dedication

To my children Kyra, Colby, and Trevor.
May your faith in God always grow,
even as it remains ever childlike.
I love you.

Chapter One

The early dawn crept across Button Up, Minnesota, like a tawny cat. After coming back into his grandparents' house from the barn, Landon Snow found his sisters both asleep in the bedroom upstairs. So Landon stretched out in Grandpa Karl's study to try to catch some shut-eye himself. He was puzzling over the tarp-covered statue and trapdoor in the barn as he dozed off. Then, in his short, fitful sleep, he saw something else.

"Melech! Look out!"

Landon sat up, panting. It took him a moment to realize he was not atop a cliff with his loyal horse friend, Melech, facing the fierce dragon Volucer Ignis. He was sitting in his open sleeping bag on the couch in the study.

Something stirred. A soft, repetitive *pft-pft-pft* sound, which Landon had come to recognize. He stood and shuffled to his grandfather's desk. When he clicked on the lamp, the final pages in his Bible fluttered and fell. Landon rubbed his eyes. Although he had read these words before, he hadn't remembered them being underlined: *Greater love hath no man than this, that a man lay down his life for his friends.*

"John 15:13," Landon whispered. He yawned. He was picturing the dragon poised in mid-flight, ready to strike. And there were Melech and Hardy and Ditty and Vates and Ravusmane and all the other people and animals of Wonderwood—or what was left of the most magnificent forest Landon had ever seen.

A glance at the clock told Landon he hadn't slept long, but it would have to be enough. There was no telling how long Volucer Ignis and the Arcans would remain frozen in that other world. Too bad Landon's friends couldn't be using this time to run away. Landon shuddered to think how close they were. His friends lined up along the cliff, the dragon hovering motionlessly before them.

My friends. . .

No greater love. . .

Did the Bible passage mean *him*? Might he have to make a choice between saving himself and saving them?

Landon had to sit down. After rereading the underlined sentence, he carefully closed the Bible. Maybe it had been a mistake. Could that have been the wrong passage? Or had his Bible merely opened to that page by chance?

Could it be chance, mere circumstance?

Landon picked up his dream-stone and placed it on the Bible. After reading in the book of Joshua about the sun and the moon standing still "until the people had avenged themselves upon their enemies" only hours ago, he hadn't expected to find another message before heading back to his friends for the rescue. Watching the engraved stone resting on the ancient leather book, Landon held his breath. Finally, he let it out.

Thunk.

Landon jumped.

Thunk-thunk-thunk.

The rock hadn't moved. Someone was knocking at the door.

It creaked slowly open.

"Already up?"

"Uh"—Landon glanced at the stone and the Bible, which were still stationary—"yeah. I'm up." In fact, he was standing and rubbing his hands down his shirt. He hadn't changed into his pajamas.

"Before the rooster has even cleared his throat." Grandpa Karl cracked the door farther and cocked his head. His eyes went from Landon to the desktop and back up. "Were you reading or, uh, testing a paperweight?"

Landon blinked at him. "I just woke up, Grandpa."

"I see. Mind if I come in?"

Landon nodded and, realizing he was rubbing his shirt, stopped. "It's your office. I mean study. It's your room."

Grandpa Karl sat on the couch and gazed around the room. Landon sat back down behind the desk. For some reason, his heart was pounding.

"Yes, my room." Grandpa Karl was staring at the bookcase along the wall, seemingly scanning each title in the dimness. "It's a room I've been glad to share with you, Landon. Along with some other things." He gazed at Landon with a hint of a smile, and then he looked at the Bible.

As if on cue, the dream-stone slid from the cover—*thunk*—as the Bible opened itself and began turning pages. This time Landon failed to jump. He was frozen in his seat. Riveted. While the pages steadily flipped, creating the softest of breezes, Landon stole a glance at his grandfather.

Grandpa Karl's eyes were wide, though not with alarm. He appeared transfixed, mesmerized. And. . .*delighted*. His mouth parted his heavy gray beard.

"It's been so long," he said quietly. "So long."

At first, Landon thought his grandfather might cry. Then he feared he would laugh. Instead, Grandpa Karl merely closed his mouth tightly, furrowed his brow, and shook his head. When the pages stopped turning—*pft, pft, pft*—Grandpa Karl leaned until the couch creaked. And he squinted.

Thinking his grandfather wanted to see it better, Landon started to lift the book.

"Uh-*uh*." Grandpa Karl raised an arm, lifting a finger. He motioned down with his finger, and Landon lowered the Bible. Grandpa Karl continued squinting at it.

"Past the Psalms, yes, and beyond Isaiah and Jeremiah. . ."

Landon looked at the book and frowned at his grandfather. It struck Landon that his grandfather didn't even have his glasses on. This was impossible! How could he possibly—?

"Ah." Grandpa Karl held his mouth open. "Ah-ha. Ah-ha. Of course." Finally he leaned back, the old couch groaning, and closed his mouth. "Mm-hmm." To Landon's alarm, he burst out with a laugh. "Ah-*ha!*" Grandpa Karl looked at the ceiling, placing his hands together, smiling. "An old man and a young man. A dream and a vision." He sighed and closed his eyes.

Landon peered at the page. It was in the book of Joel. It was a page and verse he could never forget: *And it shall come to pass afterward, that I will pour out my spirit upon all flesh; and your sons and your daughters shall prophesy, your old men shall dream dreams, your young men shall see visions.*

Landon was feeling a bit dizzy. His close escape from Volucer Ignis, his discovery of the huge figure in the barn, a very short night—or morning, rather—of sleep, the verse in John 15, and now his grandfather knowing something he couldn't possibly see.

"How did you do that, Grandpa?" Landon asked, pressing the thin page with his finger. "You can't see the words, can you?"

Again Grandpa Karl laughed. "Goodness, no. I had to squint just to see the thickness of the book. That's what I was looking at." He gave Landon a friendly smile. "Figuring out how many pages were on either side to gauge which book we were in."

Landon looked at the book's edges.

"Remember, I'd had that Bible a lot longer than you have. With my glasses on, I can tell pretty quickly where we might be, although I don't always get it right. This one, in the end, proved easy—or at least obvious to me. I was right, wasn't I?" A question mark creased his forehead, and he began to recite the verse. Landon joined in and they finished together: *"Your old men shall dream dreams, your young men shall see visions."*

Grandfather and grandson smiled at each other.

"So," Landon started, "did you go on adventures, too? To other places and—"

Grandpa Karl raised his finger. "Oh!" His finger waved in warning. "Your journeys aren't over yet, are they?"

Landon tilted his head.

"Then you best not tell me about them. Yes, I've had my adventures. Oh, yes. I've thought about writing them down someday, you know. And I was about to start doing just that oh, about two years ago, when I had a dream."

Landon leaned closer. Chills were slowly climbing his back like tiny fingernails inching toward his neck. When he opened his mouth, a hoarse, croaky sound came out. "What was the dream about, Grandpa?"

"I was sitting in that chair, planning to type on that typewriter"—he pointed past the Bible to the old, idle machine coated with dust—"and trying to come up with a catchy first sentence. Well, I'd been sitting too long, and I should have had coffee instead of tea—tea always makes me drowsy, you know— when I started to drift off to sleep. Oh, and I guess I should say, I had this guy"—he reached into his bathrobe pocket and withdrew a figurine; it was a dark chess knight—"sitting on the desk. I don't remember why he was there." Grandpa Karl looked at the knight and then deposited it back in his pocket.

Melech! Landon thought. But he didn't want to interrupt. "Go on. About the dream."

Grandpa Karl seemed to have drifted, at least in his thoughts. "Oh, yes. Well, I fell asleep in that chair, and all of a sudden there was this knight—no, not this one in my pocket but a giant one, bigger than any chess piece I'd ever seen. And, well, that was it. I never got around to writing my story. I've been too busy with this project ever since."

Landon's shoulders sagged. "That's *it*? That was your dream,

Grandpa? Just. . .a big knight?"

Grandpa Karl tensed his face. "Well, yeees. And no. That was basically it, as far as the dream. But when I woke up, I knew that I was supposed to build this knight somehow. And I saw the knight sitting—or standing—on a giant square. The only giant square I knew was in the barn, in the floor. Huge trapdoors to a deep cellar. Hasn't been used, or even opened, in I don't know how long. I'd forgotten about it, really, until this dream. So I swept it off, and sure enough: perfectly square.

"The next thing was how to keep it from your grandma. How could I spend hours each day out in the barn sculpting a big horse head? I didn't want to lie to her. I also didn't want to tell her about it. Had a feeling she might think I'd gone off the deep end."

Grandpa Karl winked, and Landon smiled.

"Keeping her out of the barn was no problem. I don't even know when the last time was she set foot out there." He shook his head. "So I named the knight the same as my other project I've been known to tinker on."

"Jalopy?" said Landon.

"Jalopy." Grandpa Karl nodded. "That old car could start if I really wanted her to, but I needed her for cover."

Landon scratched his head. "That night when you got hurt after you gave me my birthday presents, I thought the hood fell on you. Is that what happened?"

"That was a strange night," said Grandpa Karl, remembering. "I'm usually pretty careful out there, but yes, to answer your question, the hood did bump my head and crunch my fingers a bit, but. . ." He paused.

Landon waited. "But what?"

"That's not how I really got hurt that night. After the minor hood incident, I was working on my real project, this knight. Still in the early stages, but I wanted to set up a scaffold to see how high I could go and figure out the dimensions. I was about to come down when I fell—sudden vertigo or something. It was strange. I bumped my head on one bar and caught my fingers on another, bending them the way they're not supposed to go." Grandpa Karl flexed his hands with a pained expression, and Landon winced.

"Yeah," said Grandpa Karl. "Never shouted so loud in my life."

"Grandpa?"

Grandpa Karl relaxed his hands and looked at Landon. "Yes?"

"That's how my journey started. My first adventure."

Grandpa Karl studied him. "Is that so."

Landon nodded. "With your accident."

"It was embarrassing. Your dad didn't think much of driving his dad to Brainerd that night, I can tell you. But I guess even accidents happen for a reason sometimes, huh?"

Landon smiled. "I guess so."

Landon would have liked to chat with his grandfather all day. He always enjoyed listening to him and being with him. And now he had all sorts of questions for him. Who dug the tunnel behind the bookcase to Bart's Reading Room? Who else had owned the Bible after Bartholomew G. Benneford? Did all its owners have adventures involving visions and dreams where they traveled mysteriously to other lands? And what about the Button Up Library? If Bartholomew had deeded it to Humphrey Snow, then who had he passed it on to? And who owned it today?

There wasn't time for these questions, however. Landon was remembering his friends trapped on the cliff, and he could feel their time of motionless safety ticking away.

"I had another vision last night—well, just a few hours ago," said Landon. He added somewhat guiltily, "I peeked at your project, Grandpa. Out in the barn. I saw the light out there and then saw you come out, and I went inside. And then I saw the vision."

Grandpa Karl tried to feign indignation, but his curiosity and excitement were too apparent. "So you sneaked in and took a peek at my jalopy, eh? And then you had a vision?"

Landon nodded. His heart was pounding again. "I did. Except I didn't actually see it—the knight."

Grandpa Karl frowned. "Oh? Well, how did you—"

"I didn't lift the tarp."

"Ah." Wryness tugged at the corner of Grandpa Karl's mouth. "I know I told you not to tell me about your journeys, but I must ask you, Landon. What was this vision you had in the barn?"

Landon looked at his grandfather, and then he looked at the floor. He felt funny about it now, as if it were too strange and might not possibly happen. What had he been thinking? He'd been going on no sleep and lots of adrenaline. The vision made no sense to him now, although when he'd seen it of course it seemed the most logical thing in the world. *The knight beneath the tarp will carry Holly and Bridget and me right back to our friends. We'll arrive in time to. . .to. . .well, to do something to help them escape that awful dragon. At least the Arcans are still at the*

17

bottom of the cliff. I don't know what we could do to stop all of them.

Grandpa Karl cleared his throat.

Landon glanced up. "It's stupid. I mean, I don't know how it could work. It was probably just—"

"Landon."

Landon paused and listened.

"I just told you about constructing a giant chess knight in my barn. Do you think that would make sense to anyone? God told Noah to build an ark, a massive vessel, on dry land miles from the ocean. Do you think that made sense to anyone? Even to Noah himself? Even with our visions and dreams, we only see a little of what's fully possible. So leave the *how* to the One who showed you the *what*."

Landon sighed. "I knew the knight was under there; I didn't have to lift the tarp."

Grandpa Karl nodded.

"And then, it's like you said about the trapdoor. I saw it open, and the knight fell through it, and Holly and Bridget and I were all on the knight, and it took us back to—"

Grandpa Karl held out his hand. "Stop right there. That's enough. Yes, Landon"—a smile was growing on his face—"that is most assuredly enough indeed." It looked like he might laugh again. "You see, *I* had a dream early last evening. Just a little nap, you know. And do you know what I saw in my dream?"

Landon waited.

"I saw a knight drifting out of the sky beneath a parachute." He smirked and shrugged. "That's it. That's why I had to go back out last night and finally finish my project. And now it's ready. For you."

"What do you mean, finally finish it?"

"That tarp is not just a tarp; it's a *para*-tarp. Do you think your sisters are up yet?" Grandpa Karl was standing, rubbing his hands together in anticipation.

Suddenly Landon felt heavy sitting in that chair. *Greater love hath no man than this, that a man lay down his life for his friends.* He looked up. "Grandpa?"

"Yes, Landon? What is it?"

"Am I a man?"

Grandpa Karl looked at Landon a long, long moment. He stopped rubbing his hands together and placed them on Landon's shoulders. "If you're not yet, I have a feeling you're about to become one real soon."

Landon tried to match his grandfather's expression, but the weight kept getting heavier inside him until he had to look down.

"Is there something else you want to tell me?"

Landon closed his eyes. Slowly, he shook his head.

Two rough, mighty hands squeezed his shoulders. "Then we'd best check on Holly and Bridget." Giving another gentle squeeze, the hands lifted.

After his grandfather left the room, Landon sat a few moments silently praying for another verse or a different vision. When neither came, he stood and shuffled out into the hallway. From a window or a crack or a keyhole somewhere, a single ray of morning light shot across the end of the hallway, pointing the way.

Chapter Two

Holly was already up. Bridget, the family's great sleeper, remained in a drowsy fog as she slowly descended the steps.

Grandpa Karl had changed from his pajamas, robe, and slippers into a plaid shirt, jeans, and brown leather shoes. Also, he had put on his glasses. Behind the lenses, his eyes twinkled brightly as a child's on Christmas Eve. He was watching Bridget tie her shoes, rubbing his hands.

"Good morning." Landon tried to sound upbeat despite his tiredness and concern over the Bible passage.

"Grandpa Karl wants to show us something in the barn!" Holly didn't have to try to sound upbeat; it was clear she was raring to go. "Did all of that really happen just last night?" she asked Landon. "The cliff rising and the dragon clawing at us just as we escaped back here? And the Bible saying time was standing still, at least where we left everybody?" She was awake all right, but her short night's sleep had made her extra giddy.

"I think so," Landon said. He pulled on his shoes, lacing them tightly.

Bridget yawned.

"Come on, Bridge." Holly gently slapped her sister's back. "After Grandpa shows us what's in the barn, it's time for us to help our friends. We agreed to go back together."

This was true, Landon thought. He and his sisters had made a pact to return after some sleep and try to rescue their friends. Before he'd gone to bed, *he* had been the one excited to show Holly and Bridget the large object in the barn. *It's a knight.* He mulled this over. *Jalopy.* And Grandpa Karl carved him! He had to admit this was pretty astonishing.

Landon patted Bridget's shoulder. "Are you awake enough to go? We'll be heading back into a pretty dangerous situation down there." Landon looked at Grandpa Karl, being careful not to say too much. Holly had already mentioned the cliff and the dragon, and Grandpa Karl's gleeful expression had hardened. He seemed to consider especially Bridget in a new light.

"Danger, hmm?" Grandpa Karl's hands moved from rubbing to wringing. "Danger. . .hmm. . ."

Despite Landon's fear, he knew he had to go. It all seemed to be part of the Auctor's plan. He stood and softly clapped his hands. Then he offered either hand to Holly and Bridget. "Come on, girls." They looked at him and smiled.

"Oh, okay," said Bridget.

Once they stepped outside, they all seemed invigorated. Pink light was washing the east side of the barn. Tiny bits of dust floated in the air like summertime snowflakes. The faded red barn seemed to be waiting for them, pulsing with secret life.

Grandpa Karl pulled the door open and motioned, with a flourish, for the children to enter. They walked into the first room, the converted garage containing the old car, the original jalopy.

"Come here to the back," said Grandpa Karl walking to the rear of the automobile. He pointed to the collector's plate above the extended chrome bumper. " 'JALOPY'," he read proudly. "I had that made about a month ago when I was ready to put the finishing touch on my *other* project. Notice the lettering."

Landon studied it, although he didn't notice anything special about the letters. The plate itself looked different from those on other cars, since it was for an antique car.

Grandpa Karl walked to the front of the car and rapped on the hood. "This was the culprit, Landon," he said with a wink. "Bumped my head and my fingers. Though not too badly."

Holly glanced back and forth between her brother and grandfather. She apparently didn't suspect a connection yet between the barn and their return to Wonderwood.

"Is the jalopy running now, Grandpa? Are you going to take us for a ride? Maybe down to the library?" She looked at Landon with a funny expression, which Landon read to mean she was just now realizing what she'd said earlier about the dragon and cliff in front of their grandfather. Landon decided to clue her and Bridget in, at least a little bit.

"He knows where we've been. . .sort of," Landon explained. "But he doesn't want to know too much. . .yet."

Grandpa Karl's eyes were twinkling again. He drew his three

grandchildren together and crouched before them. His eyes danced from one to another. "Who did you think left the library door unlocked for you that morning last fall?" His mouth half curled into a mischievous grin.

Bridget took a half step back, the fog lifting from her weary brain. "Grandpa?" Her eyelids fluttered. She looked about the room at the old car, at her brother and sister, and then at her grandfather as if wondering how in the world she'd gotten here. "You have a key—*to the library*?" She said this in a tone of hushed reverence.

Grandpa Karl straightened. "Well, I leave the bookcase open only at night, and since you all slept through the night, I had to offer another means, as it were."

Holly gasped. She turned quickly, her blond hair whisking Landon's chin. "He knew all along?" She pointed accusingly first at her grandfather and then at her brother. "And you *knew* he *knew*?" Her finger shot back and forth. She was breathing huffily. She couldn't stand being left out of the loop. This was the funniest thing Landon had seen all morning. Holly's frustrated face could make him laugh anytime.

"He's had dreams," Landon said simply. "Right, Grandpa?"

Grandpa Karl nodded. "Dreams."

Since Holly was still glaring at Landon, he continued. "And he went on journeys of his own when he was younger. When *he* owned the Bible."

Grandpa Karl put his hands on his hips and seemed to stare off into the distance. "A boy of visions."

"So he doesn't know everything," said Landon. "He doesn't

want to. Our adventure isn't finished yet." *But mine will be soon if I have to give up my life,* he thought.

Bridget touched the automobile hesitantly, as if her fingertip might provoke it to jump. "Is this what you wanted to show us, Grandpa?" A hint of doubt tugged at her voice.

Grandpa Karl's hands were together, rubbing. "Nah," he said playfully. "Not really. It's in here." He waved them over to the interior door.

Holly gave Landon a final long squint, to which he shrugged. When they moved to the door that Grandpa Karl had opened, Landon pointed and warned, "Watch out for the puddle. It's lacquer, I think."

Holly stretched her leg over the gooey black puddle on the floor near the doorway, and Landon pursed his lips hard to keep from laughing at her face.

Bridget sidestepped the puddle and tiptoed over other little black wet spots.

When they were all inside the large room, Grandpa Karl switched on the light.

For Landon, seeing the knight's shape beneath the tarp was entirely different this time. It was more real. It felt. . .*heavier*. And having his sisters there with their grandfather took away all the mystery and anticipation he'd experienced earlier. Then his eyes drifted to the outline of the trapdoor in the floor. The heaviness he felt inside dropped right to the floor. His feet felt like sandbags. A lump bulged in his throat. He gulped.

"What is it?" Bridget asked finally.

"This is Jalopy, too." Grandpa Karl grinned. "Or Jalopy II,

as the case may be. Come on over, and I'll introduce you to her."

"*Her*?" Landon's voice squeaked. "It's a her? How do you—I mean, how can you *tell*, Grandpa?" The words sprung out, and now Landon felt his face flushing warmly.

Grandpa Karl paused and turned, clearing his throat, the boyish grin still on his face. "Well, Landon, I wasn't sure until right near the end when I stamped in her name. And then I knew. I just knew she was a girl. She's a filly, all right."

Landon shook his head. Thankfully, his sisters remained quiet on the subject. He didn't know why it seemed such a big deal. But he'd never imagined a chess knight—or any other piece other than the queen—as a girl.

Grandpa Karl reached the tarp, crouched, and lifted. For a moment, Landon felt another flash of embarrassment at his grandfather's uncovering a girl, but what was revealed was only a dark, curved, wood casing.

"See there? I copied the lettering from the plate. The 'II' I added freehand."

A flat rectangle had been cut from the rounded edge, with the letters JALOPY II etched in bas-relief.

"But what is this?" Holly asked. "It's not a car."

Grandpa Karl stretched out the canvas. "Here. Everyone take hold. We'll unveil her together. On the count of three. One, two, three!"

The foursome stepped back, drawing the vast cloth with them. It caught momentarily on the pointy ears and then came snapping off, fluttering down with a whoosh.

Holly and Bridget gasped before emitting a long, moaning, "Ooohhh" together.

Startled by the height of the knight and her brilliant, deep-brown sheen beneath the lofty lights, Landon felt his knees buckle. He stumbled backward as the tarp continued to settle in a heap. He was thrust back to the giant chessboard where he had faced the towering king. *Mate in three moves!* To be rescued at the last instant by a knight nearly identical to this one.

"Melech!" Landon shouted despite himself. "I mean—wow, Grandpa Karl!" He struggled to recover himself. "She's. . .she's *beautiful.*" Immediately he regretted saying it, as if he were betraying Melech somehow. Seeing this giant knight stirred up all sorts of strange emotions.

Something stirred beneath them. A faint wisp of steam or fog issued from the crack along the edge of the trapdoor. The floor seemed to hum.

"Do you feel that?" Bridget exclaimed, her brown eyes flaring.

Grandpa Karl appeared stunned. "It's never done *that* before!" He frowned at the trapdoor, tentatively tamping it with his foot.

"What's going on?" said Holly. "What is this place, Grandpa?"

"It's just the barn," he said. "I–I'm not sure what's happening. The cellar's been empty for years. At least so I thought." He wrinkled his nose like a bunny. "Is something *burning* down there?"

A gear shifted inside Landon. He whispered in a tight voice too soft for anyone else to hear, "Volucer Ignis." He closed his eyes, powerful emotions welling up. *Melech, Ditty, Hardy, Vates. . .* "It's time," he said louder. "Do you know how to open the door, Grandpa?"

Grandpa Karl was still busy sniffing and stamping. He

glanced up. "Huh? What's that?"

"The trapdoor," Landon repeated. "Can you open it?"

The grin and twinkling eyes had faded from Grandpa Karl's face. He seemed to be second-guessing himself. This wasn't a game, after all. Landon could see the worry overtaking his grandfather. He went over to him, clearing folds of canvas. The thrum from the floor grew stronger.

"We have to go, Grandpa. It's time." Landon gulped down his own mounting fear. "Our friends are waiting. They need us." *Greater love hath no man. . . .*

Grandpa Karl scowled. He started shaking his head. But as he gazed into Landon's eyes, something else came over him. His headshake turned slowly into a nod.

"Okay," he said, though Landon could barely hear him. Seeming to grasp the uselessness of talking, Grandpa Karl forced a smile and mouthed the word again: *okay.*

Fighting back tears, Landon said, "Grandpa, I love you."

His grandfather paused and stared at his grandson a long moment. Did he understand what Landon had said? Could he hear him? Did he understand what this might mean? Had he had a dream he wasn't sharing with them?

Grandpa Karl resumed nodding. He mouthed some words to Landon. Did he say "I love you"? Or was it something else? There wasn't time or quiet enough to find out.

Landon hugged his grandpa hard. The old man felt like a tree. A tree that moved and had a heartbeat and hugged back. *And tell Grandma I love her, too. And*—Landon could hardly finish his thought—*and my mom and dad. Tell them I love them.*

That I am doing my duty and am glad for it.

Landon knew that though Grandpa Karl couldn't hear his thoughts, the Auctor could. He would let Landon's parents know somehow. What had to be done, had to be done.

Landon pulled away, avoiding his grandfather's gaze. He hesitated an instant before grabbing his sisters. Should he take them with him? A voice seemed to say yes, it would be okay.

At least for his sisters.

So Landon held their hands and helped them climb onto the knight's back. Grandpa Karl had carved some nice grooves for the mane, which helped as hand- and footholds. And Landon noticed something else. The tarp was still attached by cords to the top of the knight's head. Between her ears, a circular bolt had been screwed into her head, through which the cords were looped.

Ouch, Landon thought, touching the steel bolt. *The poor girl's going to wake with an awful headache. . .if she does awaken as Melech did.*

Landon looked down at Grandpa Karl. He felt like a pilot preparing for takeoff. Or a skydiver readying to take a leap. He gave his grandfather a thumbs-up.

Grandpa Karl returned the gesture and moved toward the wall, where a rusty old lever protruded. Landon couldn't help thinking that it looked as though his grandfather was about to flush a toilet. And indeed, when Grandpa Karl finally managed to plunge the lever (it really must have been rusted as it seemed to take a lot of time and effort, and Grandpa Karl was no wimp), the last thing Landon heard was a great gurgling swish.

Chapter Three

T
hough the air was filled by the gurgling, whooshing, swishing noise, nothing about it was wet. It was a dry mist. Cloudy, but not moist. Then they began the spin.

"Hoooold onnn!" Landon shouted through the tornado. He was pretty sure Holly and Bridget were still there. He thought he felt hands other than his own grasping the steel eyebolt. Thank goodness Grandpa Karl had put it there! Without that ring—which was large enough for at least three hands—and the now-taut cords stretching up from its top, there was no way anyone could hold onto the knight. The children would have been thrown from her immediately, winding up who knows where.

Wait a minute, Landon thought. *How can a knight be a girl? That's impossible, isn't it? So what would she be then? A lady?* No. That didn't sound right. Ohhh, it was too difficult to think. He was getting a dizzy headache. She would just have to be a girl knight.

The cords were getting twisted.

"Ow!" Bridget squealed. "My hand!"

Landon felt his own hand being pulled inward, wrenching his arm. The velocity of the whirlwind was too great to risk letting go. But he didn't think he could stand the pain much longer himself.

Landon closed his eyes and prayed. Before long, a calm came over him, and then the ropes untwisted themselves.

A fluttering, snapping sound came from above, as from a huge flag flapping in the wind. Landon's stomach dropped as the knight lifted, seemed to pause, and then drifted leisurely through the air. They were immersed in mist as if traveling through a cloud. The tarp had opened overhead, although it was hidden by fog.

Landon stretched one aching hand and then the other. That's when he heard Holly counting.

". . .158, 159, 160!" Holly's eyes were squinched shut, but now she opened them. She looked around, breathing deeply.

"What on earth were you counting?" Landon asked.

"Time," she said. "Seconds. Keeps me distracted from. . ." She paused.

"Pain?" offered Landon.

Holly nodded.

Bridget whimpered. "I'm afraid, Landon. That was scary."

Holly glanced at her sister. "That, too. Fear. Counting helps keep it away." She gazed at Landon, a vulnerable look in her eyes.

"I think the scary part is over," Landon said, forcing a soft smile at Bridget. *At least for now,* he added silently.

Holly had rarely admitted to being afraid before. Of anything. Now Landon realized counting had probably given Holly comfort other times, too. It was her way of handling her emotions, whether good or bad.

In another situation Landon might have teased her about it. But this didn't seem the time for teasing. Landon simply wasn't up to it.

The three of them clung quietly to the knight for what seemed several minutes. The mist swirled gently up around them, and there was no fear of the cords becoming twisted again.

Finally, Holly spoke. Apparently she had finished counting. "Where do you think we'll come down? Right back on the cliff?"

"And what will we *do* then?" asked Bridget. "How can we stop that awful dragon?"

Landon thought about it. "It's hard to say where we'll come down, Holly. I just hope—" He bit his lip.

His sisters looked at him, tilting their heads. "What?" said Holly.

Landon sighed. "I just hope we *are* returning to the cliff." A funny frown came over his face.

"You mean we could land back in the valley?" Holly straightened her head and looked off into the mist. "I hadn't thought of that. What if we miss the cliff altogether? How will we get back up there to help?"

Landon shook his head. He wasn't worried about missing the cliff. At least not yet. There was something else nagging at him, and he couldn't figure it out.

"I hate that dragon," Bridget mumbled. "I hope we land right on top of him! Squash!" She shriveled her face like a shrunken jack-o'-lantern.

An electric current ran up Landon's spine.

"That's it," he said, the top of his head tingling.

Holly leaned in excitedly, her blond hair flying amid a sudden gust, and Bridget's face unwrinkled. "It is?" said Bridget. "We get to squash him?"

Landon's thoughts were elsewhere. Hoisting himself to the top of the knight's head, keeping one hand on the eyebolt, and quickly grabbing the knight's left ear, Landon peered down the long wooden muzzle. The mist was clearing. Below lay a land of perfectly tiny squares. Dark and light. Completely flat. Stretching forever.

Landon slowly slid back toward his sisters and pressed his toes into a groove of the knight's carved mane. He grasped the steel ring with both hands, blowing out a long, ponderous sigh. Holly and Bridget stared at him.

"What is it?"

Landon gazed blankly at the knight's dark brown wood. "Grandpa did a good job. Jalopy II will fit right in."

His sisters frowned. "What?" said Holly. "Fit right in? Landon, you're not making sense. What did you see?"

"I'm getting scared," said Bridget. "And my arms are tired."

Landon raised his head. "We're going to land on the chessboard," he said, "where I almost got squashed by the dark king."

Bridget didn't move, her fearful expression hardening. Holly was craning her neck, trying to peer down. "The chessboard?" she was saying. "With pieces? Where you met Melech when he was—"

"A knight," Landon said. "Like Jalopy. Looks like we're

bringing her in to replace him." He shook his head. Of all the strange places he'd been, he never would have guessed he'd be coming back here!

Holly lunged this way and that. "I've got to see this! There! There's the board! But where are the pieces?"

Though Landon was still lost in his thoughts, amazed at the notion of this surprising return, he noticed his hands were jiggling. "Holly," he said, his eyes growing wide. "Holly!"

"What? I'm trying to—"

"Stop moving! The ring's coming out!"

"The ri—oh!"

"Bridget," Landon said calmly, gazing into his youngest sister's brown eyes. "I know your arms are tired. So are mine. But you're going to have to hang on even tighter pretty soon. The knight's going to drop, I'm afraid." Landon gritted his teeth. He wished he hadn't said that last part, although it was true enough. He *was* a little afraid.

Holly was studying the ropes rising from the steel ring. "Maybe," she said, her eyes traveling up and down. "Maybe Bridget could climb on top and sit between the ropes?"

Landon looked. There might be just enough room for one small person to sit, holding a rope at either side. Sort of like sitting on top of a small tire swing. He glanced at Bridget. "You want to try it?"

She nodded, trying to act brave.

"Okay then," Landon said quickly. The ring was beginning to separate from the knight, revealing the steel screw. "Up you go!"

Bridget pulled while Landon and Holly each held and propped

one of her feet. First Holly let go and then Landon as Bridget lifted her legs over. As soon as she was seated and grasping the ropes, Landon and Holly took hold of the ring with both hands.

They were just in time.

Without further warning, the bolt slid loose, and the knight dropped from beneath them.

Landon and Holly were hanging on for their lives.

An eternal moment later, an explosive smack shot up from the board. Jalopy II had landed.

For Landon and his sisters, it seemed they were merely hovering, floating, only barely falling without the weight of the knight pulling them down.

"Hook your fingers together, Holly!" Landon spoke firmly but not loudly as there was no need to yell.

"Twenty-one," said Holly. "Twenty-two. Twenty-three. . ."

Landon looked and saw she had reacted to his command. Her fingers were interlaced as his were over the ring. It was a good thing Bridget was sitting on top. Not only might she have fallen soon after the knight, but also each of her legs served as a buffer between Landon and Holly and the spiral metal threads of the screw. The squares on the board below were no longer tiny, but they were not growing fast enough for Landon's liking. This descent would take forever. He prayed for strength for Holly and himself.

A sudden wind blew. Not from below, but from the side. The squares were gliding by. Toward the horizon appeared a small ridge. The land was not entirely flat! As they sailed closer, however, the ridge began to break apart. It was not a solid raised mass but several individual pieces.

"Forty-nine. Fifty. Fifty-one. . ."

"Landon?"

Landon glanced up. Bridget was staring down at him and Holly. Or rather, she was staring at their hands.

"Are you okay?" Bridget's voice was soft as the breeze, careful not to disrupt Holly's counting.

Landon wished she hadn't asked. The objects on the board had distracted him. Now he remembered his hands, and the ache went from numbness in his fingers to deep throbbing in his shoulders.

"I'm okay," he whispered back through clenched teeth, trying to hide his grimace beneath a grin.

Bridget nodded, although she appeared unconvinced.

"Look over there." Landon pointed with his chin. "Down on the board." It was amazing how many words he could speak without parting his teeth.

"Eighty—whoa! What are those things?" Holly's eyes flared. "Do you guys see those down there?"

All three children stared. Landon's shoulders were growing tingly and numb, which he didn't take as a good sign, but at least the dull pain was subsiding. When the objects on the board became recognizable shapes, all three children spoke at once.

"Chess pieces."

At either end of the formation stood two dark rooks like battlements at the corners of a castle. One knight stood near the left end; the knight's place on the right side was empty.

Landon gulped, his chest filled with a different sort of ache. *Melech*, he thought. *That must be your spot.*

Closer toward the middle rose the funny shapes of the bishops, and standing tallest in the center were the queen and the cross-topped king.

The children continued to sail, and as they flew over the giant pieces, another, shorter rank came into view. The pawns.

When the formation was behind them, Holly asked, "Did you hear that?"

"Hear that?" said Landon. "Hear what?"

"Voices," said Holly. "When we were practically on top of them, I could hear voices. Murmuring or whispering, like they were trying to keep quiet so we wouldn't hear."

Landon swallowed again. He'd woken in the middle of the night on more than one occasion over the last year and a half, trembling from the dark king's booming voice: "Mate in three moves!"

"I thought I heard something, too," Bridget said faintly. "Can they see us? They don't even have eyes. Well, except the knight."

"There was only one knight," said Holly, gazing knowingly at Landon. "The other one's missing."

"That's because he saved me and was thereby banished from the board. We jumped together from the corner. That's how I got to Wonderwood. We landed at the top of the cliff—the same place we left Melech and everyone else back there."

"You jumped from a corner?" Holly said, turning her head. "*What* corner? I don't see an end to this place."

"More pieces!" said Bridget. "Look!"

"What? Where. . .*oh*. . ."

Another set of ranks appeared on the board, although they were harder to see because of their light coloring, which blended with the hazy backdrop beyond the board. The children were approaching the giant pawns nearly head-on. They had descended more rapidly following their dark-chess-pieces flyover.

"We're about to land," said Landon, wondering if his legs were up for it.

"It's a good thing," said Holly, "because my arms are about to fall off!"

The squares of the board were huge, each one larger than the floor in any of the children's rooms.

"We're going to have to run as soon as we hit," said Landon. "And Bridge? You should probably jump off this thing before the screw catches against the wood and throws you. Can you do that?"

"Okay," said Bridget. "Look out!"

The floor appeared to rise at them as a sudden downdraft took them toward it.

"Run, Holly!" shouted Landon, churning his own legs in preparation for touchdown. "Get ready to jump, Bridge!"

Thank goodness he and Holly were facing the direction they were moving. Had they approached the board facing backward, they most surely would have broken their backs or cracked their skulls. Landon was running, and his feet appeared to be connecting with the floor, although he had lost sensation throughout much of his body.

Bridget hollered, "Let go! Let go!"

Landon glanced up to see his hands still clasped around the steel ring. "I can't!" he yelled, horrified. "I can't feel anything!"

Holly was panting as she ran alongside him. She was staring straight ahead and mouthing numbers, counting her steps. Her arms rose straight up, also locked onto the ring. If their situation hadn't been so alarmingly absurd, it would have been hilarious seeing brother and sister running together like that, a giant screw between them.

"You're hurting my legs!" Bridget whimpered.

"You've got to help us," Landon puffed between breaths. "Pry off our fingers!"

Bridget could release only one finger at a time using just one of her hands while she held the rope with the other. "I've almost got Holly's off," she muttered. "Just this one. . .last. . .pointer. . . finger. . ." She groaned and grunted. "There!"

Holly disappeared.

Landon glanced back and then looked down to see his sister sliding facedown just behind him, her arms outstretched like a torpedo. "That's right," he said aloud. "This board is slippery!" So they had been hardly running at all, merely cycling the air while the sailing para-tarp pulled them ahead.

The row of sphere-headed pawns loomed appallingly close. "Cut me loose!" said Landon. "Cut me loose, Bridget!"

"*Cut* you?" squealed Bridget. "I don't want to—"

"You know what I mean!"

Though Landon felt nothing, his sister must have been doing her job. Without warning, Landon fell flat on his face and noticed the wood changing color beneath him—dark, light, dark, light. Brown, cream, brown, cream. He wished he knew how Bridget was faring, but he couldn't look up to see. He pushed the toes of his shoes against the floor and began slowing down. Thank goodness for rubber soles! The resulting screech was more than an entire basketball game's worth of skids and pivots and toe-stops on the gymnasium floor.

Landon hit a wall. Except it wasn't a wall. After resting a few moments and then slowly testing out his fingers, arms, and legs, Landon looked up. Blotting out the sky was a huge orb of wood. From somewhere beyond the enormous pawn came Bridget's voice.

"Help, Landon! Help me!"

From the other direction, somewhere back along the board where they had been sliding, came Holly's voice. She wasn't shouting any words. She was screaming.

Chapter Four

After Holly's screams came her words: "They're after me! I can't move! Help!"

Landon spun on his belly to see a nightmare come to life. He could barely see Holly lying out there on her stomach. Dominating the scene were the dark pawns, clearly on the move. One would slide forward, and then another, and then another. In segmented fashion, the entire line of pawns advanced on his sister.

"Bridget!" Landon hollered over his shoulder. "What's wrong?" He had to make a decision based on the gravity of each girl's situation.

"I'm stuck! On top of a statue!"

A few more moves and the brown pawns would be on top of Holly.

Landon stood. He gained no traction to speak of, but at least he was able to keep his balance. And he could slide his feet, sort of like being on an ice rink.

"I'm coming, Holly!" About the only thing he could do was try to push her out of the way and then hope that he could get away, too. He'd thought about pushing off from the light pawn and torpedoing back to Holly, but the danger was he'd either zip right past her or bump too hard into her, sending her straight toward the pawns. To add to his horror he saw other dark pieces advancing behind the pawns. At least they were waiting for the smaller, slower pawns rather than breaking through and charging ahead.

A thought struck Landon. Where was Jalopy II? Could she move? Might she come to their rescue? Somehow, they needed to get to the corner of the board where he and Melech had made their leap long ago.

"Hold on, Holly! I'm coming!"

A voice came from behind Landon, and it wasn't Bridget's.

"Well, if this isn't both absurd *and* uncouth! Look at them. They're on the move again. The whole lot of them. Coming at us en masse. Whatever happened to one piece, one move, wait your turn to move again? Thank you very much. The gall of that team."

"They're not a team any longer, and that's the problem. They've become board-thirsty *barbarians*. That—and they're still missing a member."

"Oh, right. The king's strong knight. I've wondered what must have become of him."

Despite Holly's peril, Landon couldn't help turning around. Was he imagining it, or did he see faint faces in the bulbous heads of the pawns? Somehow they were talking with one another. And they didn't seem pleased with the opposing dark pieces.

From his new vantage point farther out, Landon could see where Bridget was "stuck." She was sitting atop the king! The steel ring had looped around the cross on his crown. The para-tarp must have drifted behind him. Landon hoped the king wasn't upset. It looked rather ridiculous.

"Landon!" Holly screamed.

"Listen!" Landon said to the pawns and any other light pieces that could hear. "We need your help. I know where the other dark knight is—the dark king's strong knight! He saved me from that king. They quit playing by the rules long ago. Now we need you to break the rules to help us. It's the right thing to do."

Landon glanced over his shoulder. Holly had curled into a ball, covering her face, awaiting her fate. The pawns were lined up just beyond her. The pawn on the far left didn't slide; it hopped—*whump!*—onto Holly's row of squares. Three more pawns and three more hops, and—

"Please!" Landon begged the light pieces. "There isn't time!"

The light pieces slowly rotated in place. They were turning to face their king. A moment later, a deep voice bellowed, "Queen's knight. Two moves. Clear the girl. Go!"

From the queen's side a knight came flying over the pawns, which were swiveling back around. *Boom—boom.* The knight bounded from a light square to a dark. It pivoted as the second dark pawn struck the square two to the right of Holly: *whump!* Landon thought he heard her squeak.

The light knight leaped. The third dark pawn jumped at an angle toward Holly's square.

Crack! The two giant pieces collided in midair over Holly, the knight's larger size driving them to the next square over. *Ba-boom!*

"Knight takes pawn!" the light king roared.

"Yeah!" shouted a light pawn.

"Hush now," said the queen.

"Knight takes pawn!" the king repeated. "Kindly remove yourself from the game."

The dark pawn twisted. Murmurs were heard from the dark pieces. Quiet fell. Then came the voice that had awakened Landon in a cold sweat many a time in the night—"Attack! The intruder is back! Attack them *all*!"

The hairs on the back of Landon's neck stood up. *Oh, no,* he thought. Before he could react, three dark pawns were in the air, converging on Holly's square. Landon closed his eyes and prayed, afraid to watch.

"Queen's knight—protect her!"

The king had responded, and Landon heard a whinnying, whirling sound. He peeked with one eye to see the light knight twirling through the air, knocking the three dark pawns away like so many pinballs off a crazy flipper. The knight came down on the corner of Holly's square and bowed toward her till its nose clunked the board.

"Climb on, Holly!" Landon shouted at the top of his lungs. "Get on!"

Holly squirmed like a worm toward the knight, took hold of its wooden nostril, and clambered up its muzzle. When Holly reached its ears, the knight righted itself while Holly still faced backward, flopping like a funny rooster comb.

Hold on, Landon prayed.

Chaos was breaking loose. The three displaced pawns only opened it up for other dark pieces to storm through. The dark queen was rushing. The dark rooks appeared far to either side, ready to assail the light side's flanks. The dark bishops had zipped out and in and out again, zigzagging their way toward Landon— and the light king behind him.

"Landon!" Bridget yelled from her post by the king's cross. Landon couldn't help thinking she must have a good view of the battle from her high perch.

If only she could jump to the queen, Landon thought. *She'd have a much better chance of a getaway.*

The king seemed to agree. He suddenly rocked, leaning away from the queen, and then teetered back toward her.

"Jump!" Landon yelled.

Bridget screamed. And she jumped, which wasn't much more than a step, when the king bumped heads with the queen.

The light pawns around Landon charged past him. Where did the one behind him—?

"Whoa!" Landon looked up as the pawn he'd slid into soared overhead. *That's right. Pawns can move two spaces on their opening move.* Not that such rules mattered anymore.

The light queen moved back, away from the ensuing fray. Meanwhile, the knight carrying Holly had also looped around toward the back as if instinctively getting his little human out of the way. As Landon watched, wondering what in the world he was supposed to do, movement on his left drew his attention a

moment before the other light knight—*the king's knight*—bobbed
and scooped him into the air.

Déjà vu all over again! Landon thought as he tossed wildly
through space. "Oof!" he landed on the knight and took hold of
its ears. They spun, leaped, and landed in the queen's empty spot
beside the king. Landon looked up at the king.

"Sorry about that ring-thing." He pointed to the steel loop
and then gestured toward the battleground. "And about that, too."

"What? This?" The king dipped backward, twisting and
turning until the ring came loose and clinked to the board.

The battle paused when the king fell backward, followed by a
reverent hush.

"The king is down," someone murmured.

"The game. . .is done."

"He. . .he *surrendered*."

"He yielded."

"Capitulated."

The light king popped back up, eliciting gasps. After
swiveling this way and that, surveying the stilled scene before
him, the light king gave a one-word announcement.

"Resurrected!"

Amid cheers and shouts and angry growls, the battle
recommenced.

The king turned to his queen and two knights, each bearing
one of the children. "Take them far away until the game is settled
or the dark king lies in defeat."

"But he won't concede, that cheat," the queen said scornfully.

The king sighed. Then Landon heard a most peculiar sound:

the laughter of a chess king. "Perhaps we'll have to wrap and tie him and bind his crown with a ring!"

Landon looked at the ropes and the para-tarp lying in a heap. He was wondering how on earth the chess figures could wrap or tie something with no limbs or hands when Holly's knight spoke.

"A dark knight approaches, milord."

The king's laughter subsided. "Then be off! And fare thee well. Return when it is safe, or return with these three none at all."

Before Landon could ask or interrupt, the three of them were off. The queen glided away, bearing Bridget along a diagonal course away from the battlefield. The two knights followed in their pattern of bounding forward twice and then to the side. Forward twice and hop to the side. As they put distance between themselves and the clash of giant chess pieces behind them, the clicks and cracks and thumps and bumps grew softer.

Landon glanced back to see the single dark knight pursuing them.

"He's back there," he said, giving his knight's ears a squeeze. "The dark knight."

In response, Landon's knight lunged ahead to come alongside the queen. "The dark queen's knight follows, milady."

"It's not a queen's knight," said the queen.

Landon's knight twitched, but held its course. "Milady?"

"It's an aberration," said the queen. "Not from here. Not one of the dark king's company. And not like the dark king's knight."

"Milady?" Landon's knight repeated.

"That knight's a she, I'm afraid, like me!"

Before Landon could say "Jalopy II," his knight teetered,

and Landon feared they were going down. The knight recovered, although they had fallen several squares behind the smoothly gliding queen. As they stumbled, Landon wrapped both his arms around one pointed ear, clinging for dear life. "Easy there," Landon said, trying to calm himself as much as the knight. "Steady now."

Holly's knight had apparently staggered, as well. Both knights were making funny coughing noises. As they caught up with the queen, Holly's knight asked between sputters, "How do you know, milady?"

The queen slowed to a stop, causing the knights to skid and bow, bumping their noses to the board and throwing their passengers. Holly and Landon tumbled, rolled, and slid. When they stopped, Landon lay on his back staring up at the towering queen. He sensed she was looking down at him.

"Queenly intuition," she said.

The knights made more coughing, sputtering sounds. One of them said, "But what about the dark king's knight? If I may be so bold to ask, milady." He tipped slightly.

"I know what happened to him." Landon's voice came out in a croak.

"Me, too," said Holly.

"So do I!" Bridget's little voice came from high atop the queen.

"Well, well, *well*!" the queen said, and Landon wondered if they had upset her. "What an *extraordinary* pool of knowledge we seem to have collected! I suppose, young man, that you're about to tell the queen that this knight took it upon himself to *jump* right off the board and banish himself from the game, all in contempt of his dark king. Hmm?"

Landon was stunned. In a voice even froggier than before he muttered, "Yeah. I mean, yes, ma'am—milady. That's exactly what happened. But how did you—?"

" 'Tis a king's business to know all that occurs in the kingdom. And 'tis a queen's business to know the king's business. As to *how* we come to know such things? That is nobody's business."

The board vibrated, and Landon turned his head for a sideway view of Jalopy II's arrival. The dark knight stopped a respectable distance away.

"You may approach," the queen stated. "I know you do not come as a threat."

Jalopy II hopped closer.

"And you, little one atop my head, may climb down and proceed by mount. The queen is not accustomed to any adornment other than her crown." The queen leaned as far as she could without tipping completely, and a light knight hopped before her to catch a spilling Bridget. It was Landon's knight.

The queen exhaled. "Now *that's* better. Consider yourself favored by the king, little one, to have received such carriage. If he hadn't borne you first—along with that outlandish halo. . . ," the queen muttered.

"The dark king's knight is a noble steed," said Landon, sitting up. "He defied his former king for good reason. He saved my life."

The queen waited quietly.

"And when the dark queen came, that's when we jumped from the board. Together."

The light knights coughed.

"Now the knight waits for us. We have unfinished business
. . .with another enemy."

"Does the knight face danger?" the queen asked.

"Much." Landon nodded.

"Does he require more help?"

Landon felt she was asking if they *all* needed more help, he
and his sisters included. Again he nodded. "Yes, milady. The
danger is grave."

"Then you shall take my knight and my king's, as well. And
you shall take this aberration—I'm sorry, but that's clearly what
you are, lass—with you."

The light knights both shivered and sputtered. Jalopy II
hopped one—and only one—square closer, as if proving the
queen's point. Not only was she a female knight, she could even
hop *a single square at a time*. The light knights appeared even
more upset.

"Thank you, milady," Landon said bowing his head.

Holly sat nearby. "Yes, thank you, um, queen. . .chess lady."

Landon heard Bridget's voice but didn't catch what she said,
as a hard muzzle scooped him up from behind, throwing him
into the air. *Déjà vu times three*, he thought, coming down on the
top of a knight. The wood was dark brown. It was Jalopy II. *If
only Grandpa Karl could see us now*, he mused. His pride, joy, and
excitement were tempered by thoughts of Melech and the others
on the cliff facing Volucer Ignis. Time was ticking away. Landon
hoped they would get there before it was too late.

Holly's knight flipped her back onto its head. Before leaving
the queen, Landon asked her one more question. "Do you know

where the corner with the arches is? That's where Melech and I—I mean the dark king's knight and I—jumped."

"Of course," the queen said. "I was leading you toward it now."

Landon sensed she was smiling.

"Queenly intuition?" said Landon.

"Of course," she said. "Complemented by the queen's prerogative. Now be off with you, and fare thee well. Do your true king proud."

"Of course," Landon said. "Good-bye, milady!"

"Bye-bye!" said Bridget. "Thanks for the ride!"

"Thank you!" Holly shouted. "And thank the king for me!"

Was it a gush of air as Jalopy II took off, or had the queen sniffed back a sob? In any case, Landon and his "aberrant" knight now led the way over the board, cutting corners as only a queen and bishops should be allowed to do. Meanwhile, the two light knights chugged through their back-and-forth routines behind them. Gradually, a formation came into view against the mist above the horizon. Tall columns arose connected by arches. Ruins, it seemed, of a great coliseum long ago.

Chapter Five

As the columns loomed closer, Landon felt the gravity of the situation grow. Would Jalopy II and the two light knights transform into real horses on the way down from the board, as Melech had done nearly two years earlier? *Only one way to find out,* Landon thought. Three more horses could come in handy. Then again, a huge, solid-wood knight could better crush a nasty dragon.

Jalopy II slowed beneath the high arch. Landon looked up. The sky was endless haze. For a moment, Landon imagined he was leaving an ancient arena after a battle. His heart told him the opposite was true. *The battle waits below.* Mist swirled beyond the board like countless beckoning hands. They stood at the edge of the board, which disappeared beneath a wave of fog before appearing again.

Clip-clop-clip. Clop-clip-clop. Three-count patterns came from behind as the light knights approached bearing Holly and

Bridget. Landon kept staring into the mist.

Greater love hath no man than this, that a man lay down his life—

"Landon? Are you all right? Whoa, knight, whoa!"

The mists swirled. Landon was aware of his own breathing.

"Landon? What is it? Are you seeing something? A vision?"

Landon blinked and looked down. He saw a notch on top of Jalopy II's head where the bolt had been. Landon wondered if it hurt. Then he wondered how wood could hurt. He tenderly touched the edge of the hole. Jalopy II did not flinch.

"That was fun!" Bridget squealed. "At first, I was really scared. Then I thought I was gonna throw up. But then it was like a ride at the fair—even *better!* Is Landon okay? Are you gonna throw up, Landon?"

Landon shook his head. "I'm okay," he said. "Just a little. . .dizzy." This was true, although it wasn't from the ride across the board. He was nervous about what lay ahead. *If there's any way I don't have to do this,* he began to pray, but then he felt ashamed. He remembered Melech saving him from the dark king and queen on this very board. Hardy and Melech charging ahead of him toward the Arcans on the beach. Ditty saving him from Ludo's spell. Vates teaching him about the Auctor and planting signs to show him the way. Ravusmane paddling Landon and his sisters across the river. Even Wagglewhip and Battleroot helping to rescue the animals from the Island of Arcanum. They had all stuck their necks out for him. And then they—and all the people and creatures of Wonderwood—had followed him to the rising cliff. They had trusted him. They would be counting on his return to help them. Yes, it was only right that he should go back—

But I don't want to die!

The thought seemed to bubble up from Landon's gut. He choked and whimpered, quickly covering the sound with a series of coughs.

"Landon? *Landon!*"

Landon quickly wiped his eyes with his sleeve. There was no turning back. How could he get back to his grandfather's barn, anyway? His destiny waited down below. . .through the mist.

Landon sniffed. "I'm okay. Really." He turned to face Holly and Bridget. It was a remarkable sight: his sisters on these giant pale knights.

"You weren't looking too good," Holly said. "But you know what?"

"What?"

"One hundred and forty-four. That's how many hops we took to get here." Holly patted her knight between the ears. The knight snorted with satisfaction.

"Forty-eight!" said Bridget eagerly.

"No way!" Holly shook her head. "There's no way you made it here in—"

"Times three," said Bridget beaming.

Holly gaped at her sister. A look of astonishment came over her face. "Bridget! Forty-eight times three is one hundred and forty-four!"

Bridget waggled her head. "That's what I said. Except I really just counted the sets."

"That's fantastic, Bridge. Counted the sets."

If Holly could have leaped from her knight to Bridget's to

give her a hug, Landon felt sure she would have. He was amazed how relaxed his sisters were. A strange realization crept into his brain as if someone else had given him the thought. *Your sisters are calm because they trust you. You're the leader, so you're carrying the weight of responsibility—for yourself and for them.*

"I read a Bible verse," Landon said abruptly.

His sisters looked at him. Landon swallowed.

"This morning?" said Holly. "Before we left?"

"Yeah."

"Well, what did it say?"

Landon gazed at Holly and then at Bridget. *I'm really proud of you guys,* he felt like saying. *I'm glad you got to share these adventures with me. Even though we pick on each other sometimes, well, I'm just really glad you're my sisters.*

"Weeelll?" Holly repeated.

Landon sighed. "It was about love," he said.

After a slightly awkward pause, Landon cleared his throat. "All right. A-*hem.* Time is running short. We've got a dragon to jump on."

Bridget's eyes flared.

Landon continued. "*I'm* aiming for the dragon, me and Jalopy II here. I want each of you to look for our armor and try to land near it or at least get to it quickly as you can. And get it on right away, okay? The others will understand. What were their names again?" He referred to the three valley men working in the stone quarry, whom he and Holly and Bridget had exchanged their armor with for dusty coveralls.

"Songbird. No—Songsparrow," said Bridget. "He's who I traded with."

Holly glanced upward, squinting. "Pitterpat took my armor," she said. "And the other one was—"

"Hedgelog," said Landon. "That's it. Try to spot those three and get our armor back. And our swords."

The girls nodded, absorbing the significance of what they were about to do—at least what they hoped they could do. The truth about where they were going and who they would be facing braced them all now like a stiff wind.

Bridget tugged at her shirt, studying it. "But we don't have *their* clothes on anymore. What will they have to wear?"

Landon knew the three men had on underclothes that looked like long underwear. Given their circumstances, Landon guessed the men probably wouldn't be too concerned about their appearance.

"Maybe their coveralls are on the cliff, where we last had them. I don't know. We'll just have to go and hope for the best."

Holly and Bridget nodded.

"Once we leave here, I'm not sure what will happen. I'm hoping your knights will turn into horses—"

"Like Melech?" Bridget asked.

"Yes," said Landon. "Like him."

"What about yours?" Holly pointed at Jalopy II. "I mean *her*. Don't you want her to turn into a horse, too?"

"I don't know," said Landon. "Maybe after we take out Volucer Ignis. Like I said, I don't know what will happen. Only that it's time for us to leave here, which means jumping down there." He gestured toward the mist below.

"You haven't had a vision of what will happen?" Holly asked.

"None at all?"

Landon shook his head. Then he paused and, for some reason, slowly lifted his gaze. Staring at the hazy sky, he suddenly laughed a single syllable. "Huh!"

"What is it?" said Bridget. She looked up, squinting. "Do you see something?"

Landon laughed again, then lowered his head. "I just keep seeing. . .a parachute."

"Like us coming down on Jalopy?" said Holly.

Landon studied the rough hollow in the knight's head. He gently traced it with his finger, half expecting a puff of air to explode from it as from a whale's blowhole.

"Yeah. . .no. . .I don't know." He lifted his finger from Jalopy II's head. "It's gone now. But I do know that we'll be falling without parachutes—or tarps—from here. So hold on tight. Don't let go. And don't try to talk. We won't be able to hear each other."

"Like astronauts going behind the moon," said Holly.

"Behind the moon?" said Bridget.

"When they're behind the moon, they can't talk with people on earth. No radio contact."

"Oh."

"One more thing," said Landon. "To break your fall—or have a better landing, I mean—look for a ridge with a slope." He motioned down at an angle with his hand. "It should lead toward the cliff. Again, hold on tight. Your knights—or horses— should know how to stop." *I hope*, he thought to himself.

Bridget cocked her head. "Landon?"

Landon looked at her and raised his chin.

"What if you miss? I mean—" Bridget glanced down and then slowly back up. She took a deep breath and sighed. "What if you don't hit him—the dragon?"

Landon held her gaze and smiled. "I have to hit him, Bridget. So I will." He took hold of the knight's ears and gave an affirmative nod.

Bridget smiled back at him, but it was a sad smile.

They lined their three knights along the board's rim. "On the count of three," Landon said loudly. "One." He squeezed the ears. "Two!" He leaned forward, pressing his chin to wood. "Three!"

Landon's stomach pitched as Jalopy II soared into the air, and then it climbed into his throat when they began to fall. Landon could only trust his sisters' knights had also made the leap into the fog on either side of him. Everything was gray and white. Wind tugged at his clothes and rushed past his ears. He closed his eyes for a moment, but preferred to have them open, barely, even though there was nothing to see.

His hands noticed it first. Jalopy II's wooden ears softened in Landon's grip until they were small, velvety cones. The wooden arched neck became a rigid backbone. If the hole was still there, Landon couldn't find it for the black mane whipping against his face. Despite his hope of crushing the dragon with a giant knight, Landon couldn't help feeling thrilled to be on a living, breathing horse! Or a living, *flailing* horse as the case may be.

"Easy girl!"

Shouting into the wind was probably pointless, but Landon couldn't help himself. She was so jittery!

"Slow down, Jalopy! Steady now!"

The words seemed sucked from his lungs into the atmosphere, left silently behind for no one to hear. Hugging her neck, Landon found his fingers on the other side and laced them together. This would be more challenging than he had imagined.

The fog dissipated, and the air brightened. This seemed to calm Jalopy for a moment. But then the moment was gone, and she was kicking and bucking and thrashing her head so violently Landon feared they might actually do a somersault, or worse, they might land upside down.

Land came into view far below. Landon thought of a spacecraft with tiny rockets used to control the pitch and roll of the craft. He loosened his fingers enough so he could use them to individually press against Jalopy's neck. Like playing a saxophone, Landon keyed his fingers up and down, imagining certain touches maneuvered certain parts of Jalopy's body. Somehow, it seemed to work. The horse stabilized and settled down. And none too soon. The earth below was fast approaching.

Now to look for Volucer Ignis. It was time to attack the dragon.

Sounds came like soft whines on the wind, but as they toned in Landon's ear, he could tell they were screams. His heart racing—as if it wasn't pounding enough already—Landon pressed his cheek along Jalopy's neck first one way, and then the other. The screams didn't come from below. They came from two girls clutching white horses falling through the sky.

So they did transform, Landon noted. *All three knights became horses.*

Holly's screaming came most clearly, being a full note lower in pitch than Bridget's, whose high-pitched shrieks sang like a mosquito's drone. Landon hoped they would find the ridge. He prayed they would, and then he closed his eyes for three whole seconds, asking guidance and boldness to strike his target.

When he opened his eyes, he discovered his prayer was answered.

The people and animals along the cliff looked like toy figurines. Landon had played with army men, and he'd seen displays like the scene below at his friends Caleb and Evan's house, who had toy soldiers of many eras, along with monsters and creatures and, yes, dragons, engaging in battles for various realms. Those fights were pretend and played for points. The clash that awaited Landon was real. Although the once-great forests of Wonderwood were lost to flame and destruction, most of the people and animals were still alive.

Before them, however, with his ragged wings outstretched, his scaly neck arched back, his tail twisted into a giant hook, and his claws extended and poised to strike—floated Volucer Ignis. The frozen dragon appeared even larger than Landon had remembered. The sight of him, so vicious even in perfect stillness, struck dread in Landon's heart.

But Landon did not quail.

As the dragon grew in his sights, Landon again thought of his friends on the cliff and how much he loved them. He thought of Holly and Bridget. He thought of his mom and his dad. He pictured Grandma Alice serving lemon bars, and Grandpa Karl glancing up from reading, that sly smile on his face. And then

Landon pictured Bartholomew G. Benneford bent over his Bible—*my Bible,* Landon thought—quill pen in hand, carefully underlining. Landon could see over Bart's hunched shoulder, zooming in. . .*your old men shall dream dreams, your young men shall see visions.*

Bart flipped the pages and continued underlining.

Greater love hath no man than this, that a man lay down his life for his friends.

Bart turned to look at Landon.

Except it wasn't Bart.

It was a man Landon hadn't seen before, although he seemed very familiar. The man's eyes told Landon that *he* knew *him.* There was the knowledge of the universe in those eyes. *Knowledge and adventure,* Landon thought. *Visions and dreams. How do I know who you are?*

The man smiled. The joy of all heaven was in his smile. His lips didn't move; they didn't have to. For Landon had been reading his book all along and had come to recognize his voice. So it came as no surprise when Landon heard these words from the Bible and from the man and from within his own heart at the same time—

For God so loved the world, that he gave his only begotten Son, that whosoever believeth in him should not perish, but have everlasting life.

Volucer Ignis emerged through the vision. Landon leaned forward, aiming Jalopy like a missile. When he and the horse hit the dragon, Landon was smiling because he knew he wouldn't die.

Chapter Six

T he crash was supposed to be cataclysmic. Landon imagined himself taking Volucer Ignis down like a spiraling biplane pluming black smoke after losing a dogfight. The reality, however, was more alarming.

Landon and Jalopy did indeed hit Volucer Ignis—squarely between his wings. Rather than falling away from the cliff and plummeting toward the remains of the forest far below, however, they plunged *forward*, smashing head-on with the cliff top, sending the people and animals lined up there flying several yards back from the impact. Some of them landed right on their feet, while most of them fell to the rocky surface. *At least they didn't tumble the other way and spill over the cliff,* Landon thought with relief. It was a strange sight: people toppled like mannequins and animals lying with their limbs stiffly stretched as if they'd been stuffed. Landon hoped they hadn't been hurt by the jolt.

The crash occurred in an instant. Landon felt as though he were seeing things move in slow motion. The dragon's open claw caught the cliff and—to Landon's horror and amazement—clutched and pulled. Rock and debris broke loose as the beast slid back. Apparently his backside and tail hung over the edge, and gravity was drawing them back. Jalopy was spread-eagled on Volucer Ignis. Landon lay hugging the horse's neck. Jalopy breathed faintly, showing no other sign of life.

Come on, Landon thought, cheering gravity on. *Take us down. Finish off this dragon! This is why we came.*

Volucer Ignis snapped shut his jaws. Landon saw his giant, lizardlike eyes blink.

Oh, no! You *can't wake up. No!*

The dragon's dragging claw tore an ugly gash in the cliff top. Landon had never seen rock tear so easily, like dirt spreading around a digging plow.

They fell backward. Landon felt his insides rise. Finally, his mission would be accomplished! He wanted to shout "I love you!" to his immobile friends on the cliff, but he was upside-down beneath the slowly tumbling mass of the dragon.

The spin continued. Landon and Jalopy remained on Volucer Ignis's back, Jalopy's hooves caught between rough, plated scales. Momentum also seemed to fuse them together. Horse and boy came up again. Blue sky high overhead. Rock wall before them. Landon readied himself for another rotation backward—like a surreal carnival ride—when the reverse tumble ceased.

The dragon's jaws opened. His neck straightened like a striking snake's. His body swelled; Landon and Jalopy rose and slid as the scales spread, loosening Jalopy's hooves. A shriek echoed off the cliff, followed by the coughing hiss of an enormous furnace bursting to life. Fireballs popped out and vanished, leaving behind pocks of smoke. Landon flinched at the flashes of light, waves of heat rushing over him.

The wings were beating.

With Jalopy absorbing most of the friction, Landon merely felt a rising and falling sensation as the vast, leathery sails soared and dropped on either side of them. The dragon's haunches crunched and released poor Jalopy between each ferocious flap.

We're riding the dragon, Landon thought numbly. His emotions were spent by this point. He should have at least felt pity for Jalopy, but he could no longer feel anything. Each wing beat brought them higher, closer to the top of the cliff. They hadn't even fallen halfway down. Landon was riding the very enemy he had come to destroy, riding him toward the friends he'd hoped to save. His only wish now was that his friends would remain asleep in their motionless state—that they would not be able to see him on top of Volucer Ignis as he charbroiled them with his breath.

Landon buried his face in Jalopy's neck. He couldn't bear to watch. *I'm sorry. I'm sorry. I'm so sorry.*

The wings continued flapping, Landon listened dully to their successive sounds: *Whissshhhh*—whap! *Whissshhhh*—whap! Something was different.

Landon opened his eyes.

They had reached the top of the cliff. His friends stood or lay strewn in a long line to the left and to the right, several yards inland. Volucer Ignis hovered, seeming to survey the scene before him. He grunted. Abruptly he lashed his head back, grotesquely arching his elongated neck. His head swiveled this way and that, looking for something. His claws, too, reached up and poked at his back, jabbing scales and skin a foot from Jalopy on either side.

He doesn't know I'm here, Landon thought, still feeling rather numb. It was as if Volucer Ignis had been knocked out and was just realizing where he was and what was going on. And he felt something funny on his back, just out of view and beyond his reach.

Volucer Ignis grunted again. Then he roared and spun about. The world whirled around as Landon held on for dear life. It was like a dog chasing its tail in midair. A funny sight, probably, if anyone could see it. For Landon, it was only dizzying.

Finally, the dragon stopped. He snorted. With two flaps, he lunged and landed on top of the cliff. Bending his menacing head, he sniffed at the gouge he'd made earlier with his claw. Then, cocking his head, he bobbed to examine something else.

Landon raised his head and strained to look. He couldn't see what had caught Volucer Ignis's attention.

"Hmm." The dragon's body vibrated. Landon wondered how long he and Jalopy would stay latched onto his sloping back. Jalopy's hooves caught the edges of two scales. One deep breath or wide wing stretch from the dragon, and they would go sliding.

"Hmm." Volucer Ignis pondered. He tapped the rock with one pointed claw. *Click, click, click.* "These marks struck both here and"—he raised his head and turned it sideways— "someplace else."

Landon held his breath. Was Volucer Ignis talking about the

claw marks he'd made here and in the floor of the secret elevator in Grandpa Karl's house?

Landon could see Volucer Ignis's eye. Could the dragon see him? The black slit slid as far back toward Landon as possible. It narrowed. Landon held his breath, motionless. The dragon's nostril flared. *Nothing I can do to hide my smell,* Landon thought. The corner of Volucer Ignis's mouth twisted into a vicious smile.

"Fim, fi, foe, fee. I smell the blood of a boy I cannot quite see."

The dragon's body began to convulse as if he had the hiccups. Low, rumbling noises accompanied the shudders. Volucer Ignis was laughing.

"Oh, this is rich. This is rich indeed!" He wagged his head back and forth. Landon noticed Jalopy's left hoof giving way.

"Somehow, *somehow* you got away from me last time." Volucer Ignis lowered his head and tapped the ground. "Right here! I clawed at you and—poof! You disappeared! Magnificent! I admit I am impressed. Yes, that is impressive indeed." He snorted. "Problem is, that deal is over. We are beyond playing games now, I'm afraid. Afraid for your sake, that is." He laughed. "And for your friends here."

Jalopy's left hoof came unhinged and slid uselessly over a rough scale. They were hanging on by one hoof now. Landon wondered if he should climb over the horse onto Volucer Ignis. But what good would that do? With or without Jalopy, there didn't seem to be anything he could do. So Landon waited for the inevitable.

"Look at them. Pitiful, pathetic creatures. It almost takes the fun away when they can't fight back." The dragon sighed mockingly. "*Almost.* At least they're still living; I can smell their foul breath."

"Well, isn't *that* ironic," Landon said. He figured he might as well speak up; the dragon already knew he was there. "You speaking of foul breath." He tried to laugh, but it was an empty attempt. "You should talk."

"Ah. So you are alert, as well. Isn't that something—that we should be the only two awake at this moment. So tell me, how did you escape? And why, oh why did you return? Hmm?"

Volucer Ignis sat like a gargoyle. His wings folded down his back. Landon studied the rigid, armlike bone that served as the wing's upper strut. Muscles twitched where the wing joined the back, an area of scaleless skin for flexibility. It was strange and revolting. Landon looked away.

"The Auctor saved me," Landon said. "He whisked me away. He's the one who raised this cliff, you know."

More muscles twitched beneath the dragon's hide. Scales rose and fell in waves. Landon held his breath as he watched Jalopy's right hoof. It looked like it could slip any moment.

"Mmm." Volucer Ignis sounded agitated.

"And I came back because he wanted me to. To. . .to. . ."

"Yes?" Volucer Ignis tilted his head.

Landon didn't want to say it. He knew the dragon would only laugh or worse.

"To save them." The words emptied Landon. Fatigue gripped his arms, and he wanted to just let go. Something kept him holding on, however.

The dragon didn't laugh. He merely echoed Landon. "To

save them." Volucer Ignis's voice trembled, and Landon felt a flutter run through the beast's bulk. "To save them!"

Without warning, the great wings unfurled, blotting out the sky. As the wings descended Jalopy's hoof gave way, and she and Landon fell to the ground. Overhead, Volucer Ignis soared, climbing like a rocket. He turned high in the air, head twisting toward earth, his body following as his wings pressed flat. He dropped toward Landon, a bird of prey diving at a mouse. His jaws opened. Landon could see the jagged teeth. At the last instant, the dragon swerved to sail out over the valley, blanketing Landon with a hot wave of foul breath.

Landon choked and almost gagged. As the stench dissipated, he heard Volucer Ignis's wretched laugh followed by two bellowed words: "Arcans, *arise!*"

The Arcans. Landon had nearly forgotten about them. Prickles ran across his skin as he rolled and then crawled on his belly to the lip of the cliff. As soon as he stuck his head over the edge, he drew it back again. A thousand arrows were racing up at him!

Rolling to his back, Landon watched, panting, as the first arrow rose up, arced, and plunged to the rock beyond his feet. *Thwick!* The arrow jutted at an angle, as long as a spear and nearly as thick. A rope was fastened to its tail.

The cord was still trailing, writhing in the air like an endless snake before falling toward Landon. Landon's reflexes kicked in, turning his body to avoid being lashed. No sooner had the rope snapped taut along the ground than other big arrows filled the sky, arcing, plunging to earth with the sound of muted machine-gun fire. Dust and grit polluted the air. Landon coughed and sputtered as ropes thrashed the cliff left and right. His reflexes couldn't save him this time. Five cords straightened overhead before coming down on him, binding him to the rock.

The ropes cut into him, burning. Landon could scarcely breathe, and every breath ached. He lay as still as possible, allowing himself to be pressed into the cliff in hope that might provide some relief. But the pressure kept getting worse.

Arcans were climbing the cliff face, Landon knew. He could feel the subtle tugging on the ropes. One particularly coarse line of twine throbbed against his cheek. He would surely have a scar if any flesh was left to mar when this was over.

The pain grew so intense Landon feared he might pass out.

Right in the midst of Landon's darkest, bleakest moment, he again saw the strange-yet-familiar man turning to him from the Bible. The man wore a beard, although he did not look very old, at least not old like Landon's grandfather. Despite his young appearance, however, the man gave Landon the feeling he had been around forever.

In those eyes rests the knowledge of the universe.

And in those eyes burns love, a love stronger than death.

Landon closed his own eyes. *I need You now. I understand I can't beat Volucer Ignis. Nobody can. . .except You.*

Tears trickled from Landon's eyes, stinging the sides of his face. It was a good sting, though. He felt a deeper love than ever before. A love that embraced pain and somehow changed it. The pain was still there, but beneath it tingled something else, something both heavy and light, something like peace and joy and destiny. It was something that neither death nor darkness nor the dragon could destroy. It was a gift from the man, and Landon was grateful.

I believe in You, Landon spoke in the depths of his heart. *I know You are real. Thank You for showing me who You are.*

The man stood and opened his arms. Bloody lines appeared on his body, and Landon felt the pain from in his own body disappear. The ropes were still there—or were they? Landon could breathe again. He felt freer than he'd ever known. The red lines on the man dissolved, absorbed by his body. He looked down, drooping, and Landon was sure he had died.

Slowly the man looked up again. He was dressed all in white—glowing, bright pure white. The brightness washed over Landon, and he felt like he was flying. Up, up, up like an angel on the tailwind of the man who now wore white. The man continued rising, speeding onward like a comet. Landon drifted back down until he knew he was resting on the cliff top. The man's distant light twinkled like a star, and Landon heard his voice speak in his heart—

I am still here. I will always be with you. Do not fear; be strong and courageous.

The ropes lay across Landon like tread marks. He was bruised, but not beaten. He still couldn't get up—but he could breathe. And that was all he needed to do for now.

The Arcans approached, their armor clicking and clacking as they ascended the cliff like a swarm of angry insects. Landon could picture their animal-skull helmets wagging like pincers on their heads.

A wind arose followed by the whooshing beats of Volucer

Ignis's wings. The dragon stormed into view overhead, where he hovered and roared. Then he dropped his head toward Landon, his lizard eyes gleaming. A smile parted his jagged jaws, revealing a pilot light of flame burning deep within his voluminous throat.

Mustering all the strength he could find in his depleted body, Landon smiled back.

Chapter Seven

Ai-yee! Ai-yee! *Ai-yee!*"

Landon kept smiling as he braced himself for the onrushing Arcans.

The Arcans, however, weren't there yet.

The shouts came from someplace else.

"Wake up! Wake up! *Wake up!*"

Despite the rope rasping his cheek, Landon smiled even brighter. He'd wondered in the back of his mind where Holly and Bridget and their horses had gone to, but he hadn't really had much time to consider it.

"We're back! Wake up! The dragon's about to strike! Grab a sword if you can! Use your claws or teeth if you can!"

The rousing call seemed to be working. Murmurs and groans and shouts and growls and howls were breaking out down the line. Soon the girls' voices were drowned out by the growing uproar.

A voice boomed from above.

"Yes! Awake to meet your fate!" Volucer Ignis scorched the air with fire, inciting screams from the crowd. Now that he had their attention, he continued in a more subdued tone.

"Your so-called leader lies helplessly before you." The dragon looked down at Landon and laughed. "He awakened me just in time! Thank him for arousing my ire and *fire!*" Another fiery blast had everyone on the ground. Landon felt the collective thump along the rock.

Volucer Ignis rose effortlessly and dropped, spewing a fire-ball and smacking his great wings to explode it into a shower of flames. *Kaboom.* Screams and howls filled the air.

"There's your appetizer of what is to come. But first, my Arcans shall arise."

On cue, an animal-skull helmet emerged over the cliff, followed by another and another and another. Landon prayed Holly and Bridget had found their armor and were putting it on.

An Arcan appeared directly above Landon, sneering down at him. His eyes were empty black orbs that sucked the life from whoever looked into them. Grotesque armor made of equal parts metal and bone shielded the Arcan's cheeks and chin, with a tapered strip covering his elongated nose. His mouth was uncovered, and a length of drool stretched and fell from the corner. The spittle sizzled on rope like acid, and it smelled, Landon noticed, like rotten eggs.

"That's gross," Landon said in a weak voice.

More drool fell, and Landon felt a burning spot on his leg. He winced, and the grinning Arcan laughed.

"You like that, do you?" The Arcan reached over his shoulder and withdrew a sword. The sword's blade was slightly wavy, and as the Arcan pointed it toward Landon's chin, Landon noted the sword's tip was forked like the tongue of a snake.

"If you thought that tickled," the Arcan teased, "wait till you taste *this*."

The Arcan raised the blade over his head with both hands. Drips of saliva sizzled and hissed. The Arcan's arms tensed, prepared to strike, when a shrill voice cried just beyond Landon's head.

"Eee-*yahhh*!"

Landon saw movement and blinked, bracing himself. A series of chopping sounds erupted—*chick-chick-chick-chick-chick!*—and the heavy ropes sprang loose from his body. Reflexively Landon gasped as if he were coming up for air after being held underwater. The ropes flew away, yanking broken arrow shafts over the cliff. One feathered shaft caught the Arcan's sword in midplunge, clanged it against his nosepiece, and sent him tumbling over the cliff with a startled cry.

Thung. Something fell near Landon with a dull ring. Thud, thud, thud. Three more pieces.

"Your sword and armor, dear brother." It was Holly. "This is no time to be lying around. We have a battle to fight!" She gave another shrill cry and swung her sword, lopping the arrows near Jalopy's sprawled body. Ropes and feathered shafts flew, some of which still bore Arcans who hadn't yet reached the top. Their fading cries were music to Landon's ears.

Gingerly, he got up. He didn't have time to tend to his bruises, although he did need to consider Jalopy. *Poor thing.*

She gave her all. Landon sighed, patting her heaving flank. At least she was still breathing, which seemed a miracle in itself.

"Landon, look out!"

An Arcan had crept up behind him, and Holly stood out of range to help. In one movement, Landon pivoted and grabbed the hilt of his sword, raising it in time to block the blow of his enemy. From his back, Landon kicked the leaning Arcan in the chest. A moment later, Landon was crouched, holding his dripping sword, having thrust it beneath the Arcan's chest plate. The Arcan doubled over, wheezing. Black blood oozed and sizzled. Landon forced himself not to gag from the nauseating smell.

"Whoa!" Holly shouted. "You moved fast!"

Landon's whole body was trembling. "Thanks," he said, "for the warning."

Holly grinned and nodded. She had mounted her white horse and, in her shiny armor and long blond hair, Landon thought she resembled both a queen and a warrior.

"Where is Bridget?" Landon asked, trying to peer past the crowd of slowly moving bodies. The poor folks of Wonderwood appeared to have wakened from a dream.

"She's briefing the others. Vates, Hardy, Melech, Wagglewhip, and Ditty and her parents are accounted for. Obviously we found our three armor bearers, and they were too confused to refuse giving us the armor. Everyone is still kind of dazed by what's going on, hence Bridget's briefing them."

Hence? "You're talking funny," Landon said with a smile. "Must be the horse and the armor."

"I've named him Ghost," said Holly, patting her horse. She

gave Landon a quizzical look. "Something's different about you, too," she stated with a hint of admiration. "You moved like lightning just then. Must be the sword."

Landon glanced at the gleaming blade. Heavy as it was, it seemed to fill his arm with strength. Although the Arcan's blood remained pooled on the ground, bubbling in hot, tarry puddles, it had sizzled clean away from Landon's sword, leaving it shinier than ever.

"It's the sword of the Auctor," Landon said, enjoying his surging strength.

Two more Arcans moved in on him. Without even looking at them, Landon sliced them down.

Holly had dispatched another Arcan herself. She and Ghost were stepping in circles, ready to defend or strike.

A spine-chilling yowl arose from the valley. Everyone on the cliff turned to look. Fresh fires were burning, spreading closer to the cliff. Volucer Ignis was on the rampage. Landon watched the dragon's black form rise in the distance like a hideous kite, only to drop and blaze a new trail of flames. Somehow even the gigantic wall around the stone quarry was catching fire and beginning to crumble. Volucer Ignis's wrath was not being satisfied through this demolition, Landon knew. He was just getting warmed up down there. Meanwhile, the Arcans were getting started on many of the defenseless people and animals. Not all the screams and yelps Landon heard came only from terror; some were death cries.

We need to get the defenseless people and animals away from here, Landon thought. They couldn't fight. And while Volucer

Ignis seemed momentarily distracted, it was time to try to move those people to safety.

Where would that be? Landon wondered. "Anywhere but here," he muttered.

Landon slipped into his armor and knelt by Jalopy. "I need you, girl. The fight is just beginning. Volucer Ignis has sent his pawns to attack, and they're not following any rules. And then he'll come, and he's worse than all the rest of the pieces combined."

The brown horse breathed heavily. She didn't appear ready to get up anytime soon.

A whiff of Arcan blood and spittle hooked Landon's nose. He grimaced and clamped his hand over his mouth. "Ugh," he said. "That smell's enough to—"

Landon removed his hand from his mouth and looked at Jalopy's muzzle. Her nostrils were flaring in and out. Nothing else was moving.

"Forgive me for what I'm about to do," Landon said. "Desperate times call for desperate deeds."

Landon turned to the dead Arcan. Using his sword and pinching his nose, Landon scooped some black tar and dipped it near the Arcan's mouth. The spit crackled, and Landon feared the ghastly combination might combust or explode. Before it sizzled away, he carried it over to Jalopy and tapped the rock near her nose. Landon crouched and waited.

In the time it took Jalopy to inhale three times, four Arcans attacked and were sent over the cliff by Landon's slashing sword. With her fourth breath, Jalopy froze, fully inflated.

"Come on," Landon urged. "Come on, Jalopy. I need you to live."

Someone screamed and fell at the sword of an Arcan, who turned to shoot Landon a wicked grin before attacking another person. The scream stabbed Landon's heart. He couldn't wait for Jalopy any longer.

"I'm sorry," Landon said to her. "But people are dying. I have to go." A tear dripped down his cheek, following the groove from the rope. "You have done your duty, Jalopy II. Grandpa Karl would be proud. And I am, too." He started to turn, when Jalopy's eyes popped open.

"That's it," Landon coaxed, spinning back. "Come on, girl!"

Jalopy's ears lay flat. Her nostrils twitched like a rabbit's. Before Landon could shout "Hallelujah!" Jalopy sneezed three times and was up on her legs, heaving. She was whinnying strangely. She sounded like an old car engine revving in waves without turning over.

Landon laughed with joy. "Jalopy, you sound like Grandpa's *other* Jalopy!"

The horse did not look amused. After another sneeze, which moved her an inch farther in from the cliff's edge, she har-rumphed and wagged her head. Her tail flicked irritably. All in all, she looked like a healthy, albeit disgruntled, horse.

Landon mounted and rubbed her neck. "Let's get rid of these nasty Arcans, Jalopy."

Galloping, stopping, circling, trotting, Jalopy carried Landon through the thick of the people. Some folks had collected ugly swords from fallen Arcans and were using them against them.

However, no one dared undo an Arcan's armor, as that would require touching one of the vile creatures of darkness. And that was unthinkable. If they had the opportunity later, Landon thought, they would gather any animal skull helmets—carrying them by sword-point—to be buried with the fallen people and animals of Wonderwood. It was not a task Landon looked forward to.

Landon reached the rear of the battle, slaying several Arcans along the way, and quickly surveyed the terrain. The rocky ridge softened to grassy plains, beyond which rose wooded hills. The hills could be miles away; it was difficult to gauge the distance.

A horse and rider approached from the right—Holly and Ghost.

"Landon! Arcans are breaking through all over. We're losing people and animals. I don't think they're up to the fight."

"I know." Landon thought quickly. "Where is Bridget?"

Galloping hooves from the other flank drew his attention. Not four hooves, but eight. As Landon turned, a wave of emotion swelled and stuck in his throat.

Melech.

Bridget on her white horse rode alongside Melech, who carried Hardy. The sight of them was almost too much to bear. Landon feared his heart would burst with joyful relief.

As they approached, however, their hard expressions drew him back to grim reality. Melech slowed and seemed to advance with extra caution. He was eyeing Jalopy.

"Young Landon," Melech said with a gentle nod. " 'Tis good to see you again."

Landon wanted to jump down and give Melech a hug. "It's good seeing *you*, Melech."

Melech took a step closer. "This is not the dark queen's former knight." He stretched his neck and sniffed, then sharply withdrew. "Are you from the board?"

Landon shook his head. "It's a long story. When this is all done"—he waved his sword at the battleground—"remind me to tell you about it. But no, she's not from the board, at least not originally."

Melech tilted his head one way and then the other. He flattened his ears and pricked them up again. "*She?* How—what is *she?*"

"Later," said Landon.

Hardy had been listening but also scanning the fight. He looked sadder than Landon had ever seen him.

"Hardy," Landon said. He meant to say more, but a lump clogged his throat. *I'm sorry. I'm sorry this is happening to your people. I'm sorry we didn't save everyone.*

"Landon Snow," Hardy said. "Dank you for coming back. And dree more horsies, too!" Hardy gestured toward Bridget. "De little lady told us what happened. To But-tin-nup and back"—he snapped his fingers—"just like dat!"

The lump in Landon's throat grew and sank, lodging in his chest. "Where are Vates and Ditty and—"

Both Hardy and Bridget half turned and pointed. A ways behind them stood a wall of bears, facing outward, blocking any Arcans seeking to penetrate their defense.

"Behind the bears?" Landon choked.

"Aye," said Hardy. "Dey're doing de best fighting from dere."

Landon frowned, confused.

Bridget leaned forward excitedly. "They're *praying*."

Landon's arms tingled. His sword lightened in his hand. "Good." He cast another glance at the bears, roaring and pawing ferociously. Then he scanned the rest of the scene. "We need to get the defenseless ones away from here. We started on the high ground, but we didn't have time to take advantage of it. The Arcans arrived before we could set up any defense. Bridget, I want you to—"

"Hyah!" Holly cried from behind, and Landon heard a whack and a crunch before he turned to look. An Arcan sank to the ground amid a growing black puddle that softly hissed and popped.

"Sorry," Holly said.

"Not at all," Landon said. "I mean, thank you."

Bridget's eyes were huge. Landon wished she didn't have to see such violence, but there was little he could do about it.

"Bridge." Landon looked at her firmly. "Get as many animals as you can around the people; fighting animals on the flanks and in the rear. Men and women with weapons next. Smaller animals, children, and mothers—everyone else to the middle and the front. You lead the way."

Bridget's eyes stayed wide open. Her mouth fell open, too.

"What is it?" Landon asked.

"Which way?" she said. "Where do I lead them to?"

Landon sat straight, raised his sword, and felt it pull and turn like the needle on a compass.

"That way," he said decisively. "To the dip between those hills."

Bridget turned and squinted. "Where—oh. I see it. Okay."

"Bridget?"

She turned to face her brother.

"You can do it. The Auctor goes with you. And take your five bear friends up front as your personal vanguard. Find replacements for them over there." Landon gestured to the protective ring around the prayer warriors. "I'm sure they could use the break."

Bridget's face softened and lit up at the mention of the bears.

"But," Landon continued, "you've got to stay on your horse. No riding the bears." He smiled at her.

"Oh, I won't get off Snowflake. No way." Bridget shook her head, wagging her brown curls. "You should have seen him take me down that hill! But, Landon. . ." She hesitated, looking at Landon and at Holly behind him.

Landon lowered his sword. "What is it, Bridge?"

"What are you guys going to do?"

Landon sighed. From the corner of his eye, he saw a dark curved blade charging him. He feinted a block but then ducked and twisted his sword, catching the attacker with a swift back swing, sending the Arcan reeling. When the Arcan stood, Hardy finished him off with a powerful sword thrust.

"Fight the Arcans," Landon said. "Until we can join you in the hills."

The riders dispersed—Landon, Holly, and Hardy plunging into the fray, sounding the retreat to the people and animals of Wonderwood, while cutting down any Arcan in their path. Bridget rounded up more bears to surround Vates's prayer crew and began leading a growing company across the plain toward the hills.

In the heat of battle, Landon kept thinking about one detail he had kept from Bridget, hoping she wouldn't worry over it. After the Arcans would come the dragon. Landon prayed that at least Bridget would escape him, and as many with her as possible.

Landon knew Holly wouldn't go. She was too much the fighter, and a good one at that. Plus, she would want to count the bodies—of both friend and foe—when the battle was over. Grim as this sounded, Landon determined such statistics were important to know.

And he'd wanted desperately to send Vates and Ditty— with her parents—on the retreat. But he knew they were also fighters, in their own quiet way. As Landon clanged and swiped and slashed with his sword, his friends' prayers upheld him and gave him the brightest glimmer against the looming darkness of Volucer Ignis.

Their prayers also reminded Landon of the man he'd met, the man of the Bible, the man who bled and then rose a shining light in the sky.

As for Hardy and Melech? Landon hadn't considered sending them away at all. They would have nothing of it. Those two would fight with him to the bitter end.

Chapter Eight

Smog from the valley drifted over the cliff. The sky's haze grew thicker, lower, pressing down like a blanket about to smother them.

As the battle against the Arcans raged on, soreness overtook Landon's arms. He and Holly crossed paths, their horses dancing a circle, before continuing in either direction. They had time for a brief exchange.

"Are they multiplying?" Landon yelled. His eyes were weary from unblinking. He was constantly on the lookout for a skull-crested helmet or a dark, curved sword.

"Exponentially!" Holly shouted back. "The more of them we kill, the more of them there are!"

It didn't seem possible, but it seemed true. Landon remembered a scene from a cartoon where splinters from a magical broomstick popped to life as more magical broomsticks. Soon, Mickey Mouse's character was overrun, unable to stop them. There wasn't time to share all of this, although the image flashed through Landon's mind in a second. He could only yell, "Broomsticks!" before he and Holly were separated by a throng of bristling Arcans.

Landon pulled to the rear, slashing and blocking and jabbing. It was sickening how quickly he numbed to the violence. He was maneuvering as if on autopilot, acting and reacting without thinking. See an Arcan; strike him down. Jalopy's hooves grew sticky with Arcan blood. Landon hoped the horse couldn't feel pain in her hooves, and that the acid-like blood wasn't eating away at them.

Every so often, Landon would spot Hardy and Melech across the battlefield. The sight of them always encouraged him. They fought so valiantly, so courageously, and so, well, *beautifully*, if that word could be used to describe something in combat. They reminded Landon that this fight was a duty. You could not let up against the Arcans, no matter how long or tiring the war became.

But there are just so many! Landon wanted to cry. And they kept coming and coming. They didn't seem to tire or wear down.

Landon found himself behind the field of battle. The clangs and cries and snarls and growls blended to a distant din. Landon's sword felt heavy in his hand, weighing down his whole right side. It would feel so good to drop the sword and then to sag and fall after it. To lie down on the ground and rest. *Just for a little while. Hardy and Holly can hold them off. I just need to rest.*

Holly's voice sounded inside his head as if from a dream: *"This is no time to be lying around. We have a battle to fight!"*

But you got more sleep last night than I did, Landon protested.

And it's this burden I feel. The responsibility. I feel like I'm to blame for all this. I just wish it would go away. Please make them stop. Make it all stop!

"Landon Snow."

Landon gasped. The battleground noises roared back on him. Had he actually fallen asleep? Thankfully, no Arcan had caught him drowsing! It was as if he had disappeared from reality for an instant or become invisible. Maybe this is what it was like for the Wonderwood folks when everything stood still—including themselves—before rushing frighteningly back at them.

Still, Landon didn't reengage the fight. Glancing over his shoulder, he noted the wall of dust following Bridget's retreating company toward the hills. *Keep going,* Landon thought. *You've got to get farther away!* For one fleeting moment, he was tempted to chase after them. He wanted to turn away from the Arcans and the fighting and the bodies clashing, falling, lying still. To get far from it all and find a quiet place by a stream—

The voice spoke his name again.

Landon turned to his left. A mob of angry Arcans attacked the black bears Bridget had recruited to protect the prayer party. The bears flailed and snapped, tearing swords from the onrushers and throwing them down. The bears were starting to give way, however. The sheer numbers of Arcans were wearing on them all.

We're eroding, Landon thought. Even the strongest rock couldn't withstand an ocean of water running over it.

Could it?

"Time to let go."

A chill tickled Landon's heart. There was the voice again,

except. . .this time it was different.

A faint shadow passed along the ground, and Landon quickly looked up. Something had flown overhead, almost silently. Stealthily.

"Let go, Landon Snow—"

Hot wind whispered in Landon's ear.

"You can't win. You can't win."

The smoke shifted overhead and began to slowly swirl. The words kept circling Landon, pricking his head like gnats.

"Can't win. . .can't win. . .can't win. . ."

Landon swatted at the air and then swung his sword. "Aaauuu*ggghhh*!"

The whispering voice laughed. "You can't. You can't. You can't."

A black bear fell, bellowing beneath a bevy of beating blades. Landon stared, holding his sword straight out. *No!*

The swirling laughter tied him like a rope. Squeezing him. Holding him fast.

"Ha-ha-ha. . .you can't! Can't! Can't!"

Another bear fell. The remaining bears drew closer. The Arcans were breaking through. Beating them down. It would only be moments before Vates, Ditty, and her parents, Griggs and Dot, were exposed to the brutal swords of their enemy.

I can't let that happen, Landon thought. His arms and legs still felt frozen. *I can't. . .I can't. . .can't. . .*

Like Holly's releasing him from the ropes on the rock, Landon felt his sword drop and then rise, slashing through the shadowy cords dropped around him by the unseen dragon. For a moment Landon feared the sword had slipped from his grasp;

that he'd actually thrown it into the sky. When he looked, however, it was quivering from his hands.

Landon stared along the sharp blade, imagining its point piercing Volucer Ignis's heart.

Does he even have a heart? What dark madness makes him tick?

An anguished cry drew Landon's attention to the prayer circle. It wasn't a bear that had cried, but a man. Someone broke from the group and was running across the open plain. The lone figure tripped, tumbled, and sprang up again. It was a small man, nimble and quick. He wasn't running so much as he was *skipping*.

"Away! Away I flee! Please don't come after me!"

But something chased him. Something small like a squirrel, zipping and rolling and zipping again, its back slightly arched like a startled cat. What little animal could move like that?

"The smog, the fog, the bog! I wish I were under a log!"

The shrill voice faded as the figure diminished. The small creature chasing him finally caught up, latching onto his leg and sending them both tumbling. But up the man popped, and off he skipped with the creature fixed to his shoulder.

Landon wanted to laugh at Ludo and his pet ferret, Feister. They weren't so funny at the moment as they were refreshingly distracting. The outburst was so sudden and absurd Landon had momentarily forgotten the dragon and the Arcans. What had Ludo been doing in the prayer group? Did Ludo really believe in the Auctor? One could never tell with Ludo, which way he would go. Except when danger got too close, then he would definitely run *away* from it.

Like I almost did, Landon thought solemnly.

Almost, but I didn't.

Landon faced the angry throng. *They're still praying back there, even as their protective barrier collapses. I can feel it; I can sense their prayers.*

Another bear went down. Landon choked back a sob. Lowering his sword, he kicked his heels and steeled himself for the charge. "With the strength of the Auctor, *I can!* Hee-yah!"

Landon struck the enemy formation, and the Arcans clattered like bowling pins, spilling to the ground. They regrouped, seething and snarling, hammering their breastplates and smacking their swords. As their swarm grew, so did their stench. They buzzed like giant flies gathering around garbage.

Landon caught a glimpse between the bears. Ditty and Vates knelt with a book open between them. Landon willed for them to look up at him, but their focus stayed on the book and on prayer. Before Landon recognized others in the group, a commotion stirred the Arcans behind him.

"Out of de way! Coming drew!"

Hardy appeared bobbing and slashing over the Arcans' helmets as Melech plunged through. Two bears stepped apart for Melech, who turned about-face between them, joining the barricade. The bears appeared encouraged by the help, roaring ferociously at their grumbling foe.

Another horse approached bearing Holly.

"I've lost count!" Holly yelled frantically, swinging her sword in a sideways figure eight to take out an Arcan on either side. "Two more! Two more! Augh!" Holly glared at Landon wildly. She appeared shell-shocked or number-shocked or both.

"Let her in!" Landon gestured to a couple bears, who parted for Holly and Ghost.

Others came in as well, as the mass of Arcans grew around them. Here came Battleroot and Wagglewhip and several stocky men Landon thought he'd seen before but whose names he didn't know. Might they have been former rope pullers on the Echoing Green?

Following them came the fighting animals. Panthers, more bears, wolves—

"It's getting bad out there!" one of the wolves growled as he passed near Jalopy's legs.

Landon gasped with delight. "Ravusmane! Good to see you!"

The mighty gray wolf lifted his muzzle in acknowledgment. "Yes," he said. Then he disappeared behind the bears.

As the people and animals of Wonderwood continued filtering in through the Arcans, Landon realized a strange thing was happening. The fighting had died down. The Arcans still grumbled and buzzed, but it was as if they had been put on hold. As men came through wielding swords or rocks or bloodied fists, and wolves slunk by bristling and baring their teeth, the Arcans merely watched, letting them pass. It was weird. It was almost more unsettling than fighting.

Something significant is going to happen. Landon sensed it in his bones. Everyone seemed to know it was time to retreat to the circle of bears, but why? Was the Auctor calling them in? Or were they being drawn into a trap?

The sky grew darker and heavier, although it didn't look like rain. The smoke swirled overhead, while everything below grew quiet. *Too quiet.* The Arcans raised their grotesque faces to the sky. A sea of tilted animal skulls above empty, lifeless eyes. Watching. Waiting.

Landon guided Jalopy back among the bears. The people and animals of Wonderwood were all together now. The remaining warriors stood surrounded by the enemy that had driven them from their once-lush forest home in the valley.

Behind him, Landon heard a small chorus of voices. "Amen." He glanced back to see Vates gently close the book. The old man stood. When his eyes met Landon's, Landon knew Vates had been visiting with the man in white from his vision. *The Auctor's. . .Son!* Vates's eyes shone with a light from another world. With a nod, Vates parted a clear path from him to Landon. Landon nodded, bowed really, and maneuvered Jalopy farther back, out of the way.

A breach now exposed Vates all the way to the army of Arcans. A few Arcans turned to stare at the feeble-looking man, and saliva dripped from their jaws, sizzling on the ground. The Arcans fidgeted restlessly at such an open shot before returning their vacant stares to the sky.

Vates's white hair was thinning. He looked tired, but strong and steady, too. Slowly Vates lifted his gaze to the dark, foreboding sky, and he closed his eyes. Somehow, Landon heard the old man's whisper, although the word came as softly as a feather on a breeze.

"Amen."

The calm before the storm was over.

Lightning flashed and thunder crashed, although the lightning was red and the thunder sounded like a rumbling shriek.

Another red flash glimmered, turning the blackening sky into a massive, burning ember. From a swirling funnel cloud, two claws emerged, followed by the tail and body of Volucer Ignis. Thrashing his neck, he threw more fireballs into the smoke, where they exploded before adding still more smoke to the smothering blanket of darkness.

Volucer Ignis turned to his army below. "Rwack! Rwack!"

The Arcans snapped to attention, heads bowed low and blades held alongside their helmets.

The dragon whirled, then lobbed a fireball like a discus thrower. The flaming orb sailed like a comet across the plain toward the distant hills, where it finally burst, illuminating the land with a lingering shower of flickering orange lights.

"Kree-*ack*!"

The Arcans responded with a deafening roar. Their shouts continued as they began tramping off in two formations, splitting around the bears and then regrouping on the other side. Soon the entire Arcan army marched over the plain, shaking the ground under each collective step. The battlefield lay strewn with armor and animal skulls, fallen friends and animals. As the din of the marching army receded, a deathly quiet settled on the land.

Volucer Ignis came down flapping, raising another blanket of dust before settling near the edge of the cliff. Smoke from the burning forest filled the sky behind his monstrous form. The dragon spread his wings and threw back his head, shrieking to the heavens what could only be a victory cry. His indestructible army was on the march after Bridget's helpless group. And now he had the final fighting remnant of Wonderwood—as well as

Landon and Holly—to himself.

With his long neck arched back, Volucer Ignis ceased his bloodcurdling cry and began drawing in breath. Smoky air streamed into the dragon's mouth like water flowing into a drain. In an instant, Landon realized what was happening. *He's getting ready for the final blow.*

Landon thought fast. There was nowhere to hide for protection. Only he and Holly wore special armor that would protect them from Volucer Ignis's fire. There was no way they could shield everyone. What could they do?

Landon drew Jalopy back toward Vates. The old man's eyes softened as Landon approached.

"It's been quite a journey, hasn't it?" Vates said.

Landon looked down at him. Was he giving up?

Ditty stood not far behind Vates, holding the book. Landon remembered when he first met her near the Echoing Green. She had saved him from the spell of the golden coin. She hadn't been able to read. But then she had met Vates, and word by word, sentence by sentence, book by book, she eventually absorbed his entire library. The book she held was the only one saved from Vates's house in the hill—before Volucer Ignis blew the hill to bits.

Ditty raised the book and smiled, her big, beautiful eyes shining with fondness. "Illumination."

Landon nodded and smiled back at her. "Light," he said.

Scanning the others huddled around them, Landon smiled at each of them as a hundred memories unfolded in his brain.

Ditty's parents—looking only slightly better fed and still just as dirty as when he'd met them on the Island of Arcanum.

Holly perched proudly on her white horse, Ghost. Holly had been skeptical at first, both about Landon's adventures in this other world and about the Auctor himself. She was a believer now, however, after descending into Ludo's tree and then battling evil shadows at her brother's side.

Ludo had already gone scampering off. Such a fickle fellow. Landon had gone from liking him to loathing him to feeling sorry for him.

Battleroot and Wagglewhip, two former Odds who, once freed from the evil shadows, became Landon's staunch allies in his quest to defeat the evil one.

The evil one is Malus Quidam. Landon had first encountered him as black shadows that would tempt and deceive and lead people away from life and light. Then he saw the shadows at work in the demonlike forms of the Arcans. Finally he met the dragon, Volucer Ignis, who ruled the Arcans. . .*and the shadows.*

Landon swung back around. Volucer Ignis must have swallowed half the black sky, although it loomed none the lighter for it. The dragon was enormous. As Landon watched the swirling black funnel being sucked down the dragon's throat, an image of a similar "dark tornado" appeared in Landon's mind. It was just like the Island of Arcanum, where a whirling funnel spun out from the volcano-like cone.

It wasn't smoke, Hardy had informed Landon. They were shadows.

His evil presence is everywhere, Landon thought numbly. *And Volucer Ignis is Malus Quidam. The dragon is the Evil One.*

Volucer Ignis snapped his jaws and lowered his head. His

eyes bulged with fire that gleamed around his pupils, constricting them to black razor slits. He had grown larger. With the swipe of a wing he could send all Landon's party flying. But he wasn't about to bother with a wing. He was done playing.

Twin wisps of smoke curled from his nostrils as he surveyed his prey. What came from his mouth was not going to be words of good-bye or screams of conquest. There would be nothing but a blasting wave of fire.

Time was out. With a heartbeat of panic, Landon spun around, crazily now, desperate to find the one he most yearned to see. Where was he? Of all the people in this place, it was the knight from the chessboard who had been with Landon from the beginning.

If only you were Melech right now. Landon patted Jalopy's neck. *Nothing personal.*

If this was the end, Landon wanted to at least look into Melech's eyes once more, rub his neck, and say, "Thank you."

Landon knew it was deeper than that. His heart ached to say farewell to his trusty steed. He could hear Melech's voice in his mind: *"Young Landon, I have done my duty, and am glad for it."*

A rushing noise hissed from the cliff. The fire was coming. A preliminary blast of heat nearly knocked Landon from Jalopy's back. The flames would soon be upon them.

Squinting against the burning smoke, Landon sagged with despair. "Wherever you are, Melech," he choked, "I love you."

Ditty bowed her head, hugging the book to her chest. Landon closed his eyes, hot tears doing nothing to relieve their stinging.

The air crackled like a furnace. Something rushed past Landon—*in the other direction.* He had to turn and look.

Against the orange glow of the oncoming fire bobbed the figure of a horse and rider, plunging straight into the flames.

"Melech!" Landon shouted. "Look out!"

At that instant, Melech fell, crashing sideways. When he clambered up again, his rider—Hardy—was gone. Something stuck out from Melech's side—an arrow? Melech stumbled on into the fire. Then he leaped.

Chapter Nine

Melech galloped headlong into the fire, leaping between the dragon's gaping jaws. The flames chased after him, reversing direction until they had flowed right back into the dragon's mouth.

Volucer Ignis gagged, staring in shock at the unscorched field before him. His fire was gone. He'd inhaled a horse. His eyes bulged. His jaws gaped helplessly, issuing nothing but smoke.

Flopping his wings like a wounded bird, Volucer Ignis beat against the ground, writhing violently. He stumbled back, gnashing his jagged teeth and snapping them like an angry dog. He was trying to cough Melech up, to dislodge the hitch from his throat. Between each feeble attempt, the dragon recoiled before thrusting out his head with a silent cough. During one of these recoils, when his scaly neck drew back and then his head rolled forward, Landon saw it: a tiny break among the scales where a sliver poked out. Landon almost gagged himself, imagining Melech inside that neck, being mashed about. The sliver sticking out was the arrow that had been shot at Melech.

Who would have shot him with an arrow?

Volucer Ignis's eyes rolled up into his head. His wings stopped pounding. His neck swung limply left, and then right, and then around to the back. His claws scraped stiffly, locked in their final grasp, dully scratching the earth before giving way to the cliff.

Volucer Ignis was gone.

Landon could only stare, motionless, his mind replaying the scene that had happened so quickly while his eyes absorbed the empty spot where the dragon had been.

He's gone. There was no more immediate danger.

He's. . .gone. Melech was gone, too.

An explosion sounded from the valley. Landon flinched and closed his eyes. He could feel it in the cliff.

They were gone. They were really gone.

Something else was happening. Landon opened his eyes. The explosion seemed to loosen the black mass hanging overhead. A few trickles of light shot through like fingers working to pry the darkness apart.

As a tremendous stillness settled over the land, Landon thought he heard the Arcans marching in the distance. *No,* something told him. *They've stopped, too. Their leader is dead!* Could it really be true? The marching noise he heard was his blood pulsing in his ears. *Crunch, crunch, crunch.*

Landon climbed off Jalopy and walked slowly toward the

cliff. Smoke still climbed from the burning valley, but it was thinning. The once black clouds above turned light gray, separating. For Landon it felt like he was waking from a nightmare—or stepping outside after a terrible storm had passed.

But it was a storm that had left real bodies in its wake.

"Melech," Landon said hoarsely. He stepped carefully around the bodies, aware of them but not really looking at them. Landon's insides felt empty. His mouth tasted dry and gritty. Fresh tears dribbled from his eyes, finally soothing their burning sting.

"Melech. . ."

A moan sounded. Someone was alive!

Landon focused on the bodies, looking for signs of life.

"Ooohhh. . ."

"Who said that?" Landon realized he was carrying his sword, ready to slash at an Arcan. He found a soft spot on the ground and plunged the blade. He removed his helmet and wiped his brow. "Where are you?" Landon turned slowly about.

"Mmmnnn*aaauuugggh*! Horsy! Giddap! Wait for me!" A hand groped the air, then fell down.

Landon ran over, carefully jumping over bodies. "Hardy! Of course!"

Hardy's mouth hung open, exposing several crooked teeth. His eyes appeared glazed. "Must stop de dragon. Must stop—"

"Hardy." Landon knelt beside Hardy and touched his shoulder. "Melech did it. He stopped Volucer Ignis. He"— Landon paused to contain his emotion—"pushed him over the cliff."

Hardy's eyes slowly focused. "He did it? Dat horsy did it?"

Landon nodded, feeling pricks of pride tickle his scalp. "Where is he?"

Landon frowned. His face contorted uncontrollably. "He went down with him. Melech jumped right into the dragon's jaws."

Hardy exhaled. "No." He sounded proud, too. "I was going to drow my sword at his eye, distract de big bugger so we could all properly attack. But to jump into his droat—"

Hardy squeezed his eyes shut, wincing, as if the truth of what happened finally hit him. Melech was gone. And he'd given his life for the rest of them.

Other people and animals had come over. Some stood near Landon and Hardy; some stood along the cliff's edge.

Vates stood beside Landon. "That was most valiant," he said solemnly. "A heroic display of courage, love, and quick thinking."

Ditty knelt by Landon. After glancing at Hardy to make sure he was okay, she turned to look at Landon's face.

"He meant a lot to all of us. I know he meant the most to you. And we all knew you meant the most to him, too."

When Ditty touched his arm, it was like a valve had been released. All the air went out of Landon's body, and he whooshed, sagging and slumping forward. But he didn't cry.

"He was my best friend. I should have been the one riding him. I should have gone with him."

Landon remembered studying the strange sign atop this very cliff with Melech long ago, a sign telling them how to get down to the valley.

" 'The weigh down is the way down, the place where two ends meet.' Melech knew the way down, and two did meet their end there." Landon shook his head.

Hardy was shaking his head, too, and moaning. He sat half-way and then collapsed. "What happened?" He lifted his hands.

Vates leaned closer. "What do you mean, Hardy? You fell from Melech, and he continued the charge alone. Did you bump your head again?"

"Mmmnnn!" Hardy shook vigorously. "Why did we fall? Melech never fall for no reason. Very stable horsy."

A shiver ran down Landon's spine. "The arrow!" He glanced toward the cliff and scanned the rocky ledge. "I almost forgot. Didn't anyone else see it? Something hit Melech when he was running. That's why he fell."

The others looked at him.

"Arrow?" Hardy sat all the way up, grimacing in pain. "But all de Arcans ran away. Who would have shot—"

"You fools! *I* shot him. And you're lucky I didn't shoot you, too!"

The shiver in Landon's spine turned prickly hot. *I know that voice. But where is he?* Landon stood and was about to move toward the cliff when the voice shouted—

"Halt! One more step and you're dead—just like your stupid horsy friend."

The voice laughed cruelly, although Landon detected a tremor in it.

"Show yourself if you're so clever and brave." Landon waited, surveying the lying bodies using only his eyes. None of them appeared to be moving. Very, very slowly he shuffled his feet in the direction of his sword.

A drumming of hooves approached from behind.

"I saw you, Maximillian Westmorelandfieldshire! *Hyah!*"

Holly and Ghost raced by to Landon's right. Landon lunged for his sword and followed. A long-horned animal skull popped up from the rock. Something sailed through the air toward Holly.

"Holly!" Landon shouted.

She had already reacted, however, and deflected the arrow off her sword.

"You'll have to do better than that, you rodent!"

Rodent?

Holly propelled Ghost right over Max's head, nearly knocking off his helmet. Max was hiding in a rift, a crack in the rock just deep enough for him to conceal himself. Holly hopped down from Ghost and stood over Max as he scrambled to his feet. He turned toward her, reaching for another arrow, but she waved her sword in warning and he withdrew his hand, empty.

"Well, big brother," Holly said. "Shall I take care of him right now?"

Landon wanted nothing more than to say yes. Max had turned to face Landon as he walked toward him. They stood six feet apart, staring at each other. Landon couldn't believe how horrible Max looked—dressed like an Arcan, filthier than ever, and smirking like an imp. Worse than his outer appearance, however, was the cruelty and meanness oozing from his soul.

Without looking, Landon sensed everyone else staring at them. He imagined Vates's, Hardy's, and Ditty's faces—their eyes locked on him. Sunlight had broken out, driving the heavy clouds away. Landon slowly tilted his sword, sending a glimmer along the silvery blade.

"Whatcha gonna do, 'fraidy cat?" Max sneered. His right hand, however, was trembling. "You don't have it in you to hurt a fly."

Landon tried to control his breathing. He gripped the hilt of his sword so tightly his hand was throbbing.

"I killed a hundred Arcans today," said Landon coolly. "So what's one more?" He flicked his sword, and to his satisfaction, Max flinched. "You look like one of them."

"And smell like one, too," Holly added.

Max licked his lips and tried to spit, but only a little dribble came out.

"Yeah, well more than a hundred more came to replace them. And now they're going after your stupid little sister. The Arcans are indestructible and unstoppable."

Landon tilted his head and squinted. "Are they? I have a feeling they've already stopped, now that their—now that *your* leader is dead."

A funny smile pinched Max's face. His eyes darted to the cliff's edge and back at Landon.

"Is he?"

Landon fought the urge to raise his sword. His voice trembled now, though not from fear.

"You're a traitor, Max, and you deserve to die."

A murmur of agreement came from the small crowd loosely gathered around. Landon didn't detect Vates's or Ditty's voices among them, however.

"A traitor to who?" Max scoffed. "I've never been your friend." He looked around. "Or anyone else's."

Holly thrust her sword, stopping a foot short of Max. "That's right. You've never been anyone's friend, have you? Who would want to be your friend?"

Max lowered his head. Rather than appear sad, however, he only glowered. His face grew dark, his brow pushing over his eyes. "I don't want friends."

Landon shook his head. "You're my grandparents' neighbor. You're a traitor to them and to us. Neighbors are supposed to help each other."

Max rocked his head back and laughed. "Help each other? Ha! What was that back in the library, then? When Humphrey wouldn't let Percy share the deed to the library after Bart the fart kicked it? Huh? What was that?"

Landon couldn't believe his ears. The Button Up Library? The Westmorelands really did hold a grudge. And it was over something they never had a right to, anyway.

Holly piped up. "The BUL probably wouldn't even be there now if Percy and your family had gotten hold of it. He didn't want the library; he only wanted more land and money. Our grandfathers wanted to keep the library open to the public for free. The way it should be. The way Bartholomew G. Benneford wanted it."

Max wagged his head like an animal. "Aarrgggh!" His shoulders heaved with rage.

"You're sick," Landon said finally. "You're sick, Max. Your whole family has been infected by greed—and something worse.

I don't get it. And I can't believe we're talking about the library here."

Landon stepped to the edge and looked over. A breeze wafted up, cooling his head beneath his sweaty, matted hair. Closing his eyes, he could almost imagine things the way they once were: Melech alive with him, just the two of them here together, looking out over the vast forest below. *We ran from arrows shot by another Max down there,* Landon puzzled. *Maple-tree Max. The hundred-to-one Odd.*

Landon opened his eyes to the scarred wasteland below. He cringed from it and turned to Max. "How many arrows did you shoot before hitting Melech? Was that your hundredth shot?"

Max looked at him with surprise. "What?"

"Never mind," said Landon. "That Max had friends, I think. He wasn't an Arcan-wannabe; he was just an Odd with the rest of them." He sighed.

Landon heard sniffing. Ravusmane the wolf appeared, examining the crack Max was standing in. Ravusmane raised his muzzle, pointing to Max.

"He's still held by the enemy. This"—he lowered his nose to the crack—"is a dragon scrape."

Vates's voice came from behind. "Ravusmane means the boy is still in Volucer Ignis's clutches. His mind is darkened, and his heart hard as these stones."

"So should I kill him?" Landon asked.

"You should do what is right."

Ditty stepped into Landon's peripheral view. She still held her book, hugging it to her chest.

"He killed Melech." Landon glared at Max.

Ditty said softly, "Did he?"

" 'Course I did," Max said smugly. "Easiest shot in the world."

Landon tilted his head as if he had a tic. *Did he? What kind of question is that? I saw the arrow hit him! But. . .the arrow didn't kill him. And neither did the dragon.*

"Melech gave his life. Nobody took it from him."

"That's crazy," Max said, looking around. "I killed your stupid horse! Killed him and fed him to my master." His sneers met only with looks of disgust.

"Enough," Landon said. As he turned his back to Max, he noticed Ditty give him a little smile.

Vates's wispy white hair flew in the light breeze. The man appeared ready to wither away. Everything about him was old and frail except his eyes, which reflected the brightening sky.

Hardy leaned away from his hurt leg. Seeing him standing magnified the ache of Melech's loss.

The black bears had nuzzled their fallen kin and now stood on all fours facing Landon. Brief though it was, his time confronting Max had allowed the bears and wolves and panthers and people to grieve their dead. Some bodies were surrounded by stones. Others had dust poured on their heads. A number of wolves had gathered animal skulls and made several neat piles. What had looked like a bloodied battlefield now had the air of a reverent burial ground.

Landon sighed heavily. He asked a silent prayer for strength, and then he said, "It's time to go. The sun won't hold still for us today, I'm afraid. The others will reach the hills soon, I hope.

I believe the Arcans have been stopped because their master is down. Still, our friends will be anxious for our return. It will be good to see them, and"—Landon paused to swallow back his emotions—"to tell them the news. Volucer Ignis is dead!"

A cheer rose up, the most wonderful sound Landon had heard all day.

"Ho, Melech!" someone shouted, and a number of voices echoed the refrain.

"Ho, Melech," Landon said in a breaking voice. Looking up at the clear sky, he mouthed, *Thank you.* And he thought he noticed a twinkling daystar. After he blinked, however, it was gone.

"What about him?" Holly asked, thrusting her sword at Max. "Are we just going to leave him here?"

Landon looked at her. "Do *you* want to take him with us?"

Holly shrugged. "No. I don't want to ever see him again."

Landon glanced at Max. "Neither do I."

"Fine by me," said Max. "Never ever again." He continued watching Landon and Holly warily, as if unsure they were really going to let him go, just like that.

Holly jabbed the air one more time, getting Max to jump and squeak. She turned away with a huff and sheathed her sword. After mounting Ghost, she never looked back.

Landon had a hard time walking away. He didn't want to leave Melech, or what remained of him, down there alone with Volucer Ignis. It was an awful place to be left. And an awful monster to be left with.

Landon looked down from the cliff one last time. "The

weigh down is the way down, the place where two—*friends*—
meet. I'll never forget you, Melech." A single tear fell from
Landon's cheek. He hoped it would find his friend.

A noise along the cliff face drew Landon's ear. Max was
climbing down a rope. Landon saw the arrow shaft securing the
rope to the rock, and he ran to it. Drawing his sword with both
hands, Landon swung the blade with all his might, hearing it
sing as it sliced through the air. When it reached his other side,
Landon looked down at the arrow. It was still intact. He panted
angrily, forcefully. What sweet revenge it would be to chop that
arrow or hack that rope and listen to Max's falling scream.

What sweet revenge. . .

What sweet revenge. . .

Landon sheathed his sword and walked away.

Chapter Ten

Before getting out of earshot, Landon heard Max's parting blow. "If I find your friend's skull, I'll make myself a new helmet!"

Landon gritted his teeth and forced himself not to turn back. The thought of Max wearing Melech's skull troubled him. Landon hoped there wouldn't be any skull left after that fall.

And then he felt badly for thinking that.

Just go, he told himself. *Go. Don't listen to Max. Don't think about it.*

But another thought disturbed him like a dragon scrape in his mind. Was Volucer Ignis really dead? How could someone who was made of death *die*?

Jalopy stood waiting, and the sight of her startled Landon. She looked so much like Melech, although she didn't talk and her features seemed sharper or harder as if she were still made of wood. Yet she was a good horse, and Landon was grateful for her.

But did he miss Melech.

Landon mounted and rubbed Jalopy's neck. "We'd better get going." He sighed. "We can't bring him back, can we?"

Jalopy whinnied softly, and Landon thought she was expressing her condolences.

"Yeah," he said. "He was a really good horse. Thanks."

Holly and Ghost came alongside them. "I can't believe we're letting Max go. I really thought you were going to chop the rope."

Landon looked at her. "So did I. But the Auctor didn't want me to."

Holly tilted her head. "He *made* you miss?"

Landon nodded. "I think so. I wanted to chop it. I really did."

"You still could." Holly raised her eyebrows.

"Don't tempt me. Come on." Landon nudged Jalopy with his heels, and they turned toward the plain.

Hardy stood helplessly, as if he didn't know what to do.

"Ride with me, Hardy." Landon reached down his hand for him and helped him up.

"Dank you," Hardy said blankly. His gaze was as distant as the hills.

Landon looked at the others and said to Holly, "Can you take Vates with you?"

"Of course. Yes."

But Vates walked over to Landon first. Unlike Hardy, Vates's eyes were clear and focused. His brow was lined with concern.

"Do you know where to go, young Landon Snow?"

Landon smiled. It felt good to talk to Vates.

"The Auctor pointed my sword"—he patted the hilt—"at the hills. Beyond that I don't know—wait."

Landon held up his hand. His nose had grown so used to the stench of death and sizzling Arcan blood that he'd forgotten what fresh air smelled like. This wasn't merely clean air he smelled, but something else. Something sweet like perfume. He closed his eyes, drawing in the fragrance. It was soothing, wiping some of his sadness and anger away.

He opened his eyes. "Do you smell that, Vates?"

Vates studied him. The old man closed his eyes and raised his chin, pursing his lips as he inhaled. "Faintly, yes." He opened his eyes, which reflected the blue depth of the sky. "It's not from here"—he waved his hand over the battlefield—"but from above. Can you *see* it?"

Landon frowned. "See it? It's a *smell*. How can I see—wait!" Landon raised his hand again, and Vates laughed softly. Landon stared across the plain to the hills. Then he saw it.

"It's a rose," he said. "Yes, I can see it! It's on a hill. And it's huge. As big as a tree! And past the hill, there's a. . .a. . .oh. It's fading." Landon sniffed. "And so is the smell. Ugh!" The stink of sweat and bodies rolled over him. He'd give anything to smell that wonderful rose again!

Vates was smiling, the happiest expression Landon had seen since Grandpa Karl's excitement in the barn. "The Rose of Shay Run. It must be. Oh, the Auctor has grand plans in store yet. Particularly for you, I think." Vates patted Landon's leg and then turned to join Holly and Ghost. A new lightness lifted his step. "Yes, this bodes well. It bodes very well, indeed."

Ditty was still roaming among the bodies of people and animals. Over each one, she bowed and closed her eyes. *What a remarkable girl,* Landon thought. She had to be one of the most thoughtful and unselfish people he'd met. Ditty's mother and father were talking with some bears, who appeared fascinated by whatever they were saying.

Landon didn't know how to whistle, so he unsheathed his sword and held out his helmet and banged them together. *Clank! Clank! Clank!* Everyone turned his way.

"Come here. Come here." Landon motioned them in. He could hear Hardy breathing behind him. Holly maneuvered Ghost to the back of the party, where she turned to face Landon.

"We've faced some great losses today," Landon began. "A lot of our friends gave their lives in battle. And Melech took the final fall for us all. It's hard to believe it was only a day ago when you were slaves to Volucer Ignis and his Arcans, working in the mine and building his wall and"—he looked at the animals—"being chased or killed for sport. What a long day! Yet it happened so fast. I know for you it seemed to happen in the blink of an eye. For me and my sisters it involved a little more than that."

Holly smiled and nodded.

"Now we're together again, and Volucer Ignis is down and his army is done."

"Are they dead?" Battleroot asked and looked around at his peers. He pointed at the skull and crossbones tattoo on his arm. "Do you really think we dropped them. . .for good?"

The others grumbled and murmured.

Landon sighed. Something told him that they really were safe and that Bridget and her company were not being threatened by the Arcans. But he wasn't sure how to answer.

"I don't know." He looked at Vates, whose intent expression seemed to say that he didn't know, either. "They've been stopped. We've won this battle. But I think only the Auctor can truly defeat them. The dragon's power and the Arcans' numbers are too great for us alone."

The people and animals mumbled, nodding.

"So what do we do now?" someone asked.

"We head for the hills to catch up with the others."

"And then what?" the same person asked. "I mean, what will we do there? We have no homes. We don't have anything."

More murmurs and grumbles. This wasn't going to be easy. Couldn't they at least be content for a moment to take some small joy in their victory?

"I know," said Landon. "He destroyed it all, and he drove us out. What we have to do now is move on. And trust the Auctor. He has given me a vision—I've seen a giant rose—and pointed the way. All we can do is follow and see where he leads us."

Ditty asked a question, her light stringy hair glistening in the sunlight. "Is it the Rose of Shay Run?" Her eyes widened hopefully.

"I think so," Landon said. "Vates thinks so." The old man nodded solemnly.

Ditty stared wondrously at Landon, her mouth parting. Landon almost blushed under her gaze until he realized she was looking right through him. *She's seeing the Rose.* Suddenly Ditty turned, first to her parents and then to address everyone.

"The Rose of Shay Run is the way to the Auctor's Kingdom." She spoke almost in a monotone, as if she were holding back all her emotion. "I've read about it in his Book." She lifted the book, which was crispy and bent at one corner from the dragon's fire.

As all eyes watched her, all ears waited to hear more. Ditty held the book high and continued.

"But there will be one final test, where each one of us must put our trust in the Auctor and in him alone."

Everyone was silent. A breeze stirred the air of the dead and carried the buzz of flies.

"What will this test be?" someone asked.

Ditty lowered the book, pausing. Finally she turned to Landon as if he might have the answer. He shrugged, and Ditty's wide eyes softened. She faced the crowd. "We'll find out when we get to the rose."

"I can tell you one thing," Landon announced cheerily. "It will smell a lot better when we get there!"

Laughter and cheers arose. Soon everyone was moving onto the plain, leaving the cliff and the battlefield—and their fallen friends—behind. Most of the people, including Ditty and her parents, rode on the backs of bears, who seemed to enjoy the close company. One person, however, refused to ride. Apparently, Wagglewhip still felt guilty over betraying his friends to the Arcans ages ago. The few who knew of his betrayal had long since forgiven him. Still, Wagglewhip chose to run alongside the group, rather than ride, paying his solitary, self-imposed penance.

They stepped into tall grass, where the horses' legs vanished and the smaller animals disappeared. The bears held their heads above the grass like beavers paddling across a stream. Ditty swayed back and forth, clutching her black bear's fur while holding her book beneath her armpit. She didn't look too comfortable, and Landon felt glad to be riding on horseback.

Chapter Eleven

As the band of weary warriors made their way across the grassy plain, the sun began to set beyond the hills.

"Won't get dere before dark," Hardy mentioned.

Landon would have preferred not to camp out in the open country, but the thought of getting off Jalopy, removing his armor, and lying down was appealing nonetheless.

"We should probably circle up, don't you think?" Landon asked over his shoulder.

Hardy's breathing came raspily, although he seemed to be recovering from his hard fall overall.

"Dat's a good idea." Hardy cleared his throat before whistling and shouting, "Wagglewhop! Hody hop!"

Wagglewhip had been trotting out in front of the company, his head popping up from the grass every so often to check his direction. He popped up now, spinning to view his horse-riding friends.

"Oh!" he shouted back. "Kay!" he said on his next jump.

Landon noticed the grass waving where Wagglewhip ran through it. Other ripples of grass indicated more movement below, where unseen animals approached.

Holly and Vates appeared to be having a deep discussion on the back of Ghost.

"That's the amazing thing, Holly," Vates was saying. "That even though this grass is here today but gone tomorrow, the Auctor knows how many blades there are and how many there will be."

"I like him more and more," Holly said. "I hadn't realized how into numbers he was before. From the hairs on my head to the stars in the sky."

"And from the grass on the field to the sand on the shore."

"How can he keep track of it all?"

Vates was smiling. "Well, he *made* it all, so keeping track of everything is part of his nature."

"So, is nature part of his nature?" Holly asked.

"It's certainly a reflection of his nature."

"I'm sorry to interrupt," Landon said. "Especially when you're talking about the Auctor. I think we should stop soon and set up camp before it gets dark. It's hard enough staying together in this grass as it is."

Vates paused to consider, looking at the sky and then their surroundings. He nodded.

"I'm sure everyone is tired and could use the rest. If not for my lively conversation with Holly, I'm afraid I might have dozed and fallen off already."

Holly smiled, pleased.

The grass rustled below Landon, and a furry gray head appeared. It was Ravusmane the wolf.

"Would you like us to form an inner and outer perimeter for the bivouac?"

Landon scratched his head. "Um, yes. That's a good idea. Thank you." He wasn't exactly sure what Ravusmane meant, but he trusted him. The wolf had proven himself as a scout, guide, and logistician when he'd led Landon, Holly, and Bridget from the far mountain across the valley to the rock quarry inside Volucer Ignis's wall. Anything Ravusmane suggested was good by Landon.

Ravusmane ducked back into the grass and hurried off. A series of barks and howls erupted around them, and then a marvelous thing happened. The grass started going down. The wolves were purposefully tramping it flat until a circle had been formed around the two horses and their riders. The black bears came in, carrying their passengers. Panthers crept in, eyeing the grassy wall warily. And Wagglewhip and some other men walked in, admiring the hasty encampment.

Ravusmane jogged around, sniffing and inspecting. He approached a panther, stopped, and growled and whined at the sleek cat, motioning with a forepaw. It was an intriguing sight, to be sure. The cat lowered his head and slunk off, purring. One quick meow had the other panthers following him, disappearing through the grass wall.

"Where are they going?" Landon asked.

When the last cat was gone, Ravusmane turned and trotted over to Landon.

"The outer perimeter," Ravusmane explained. "A few of

my comrades and I will also be making the rounds. So far, I've picked up no enemy scent." He paused, twitching his ears. "It's peculiar. I could smell the Arcans until the moment Volucer Ignis fell from the cliff. I'm certain we could have been trailing their scent, which I believe was in the direction we've been heading, had it not been erased."

"Erased?" Landon said uneasily.

"Well, just that it's gone," said Ravusmane.

"Hmm. And their movement? That stopped, too, didn't it? I mean, they stopped marching when the dragon fell, right?"

Ravusmane nodded, turning his head to survey the campsite. "Apparently so."

Landon guessed Ravusmane was also perplexed by this. But Landon was glad for it, mysterious as it was. It meant the Arcans weren't still advancing on Bridget and the others.

"We'll check it out tomorrow," said Landon. "See if we can find any clues to what happened to them. Or if they all just disappeared when the dragon. . .fell." He still couldn't get himself to say *died*, although he hoped that's what had happened.

As people and animals alike began to bed down, finding spots to stretch out or collapse for the night, Landon stood with Vates, Hardy, and Holly near the horses.

"I can't believe I'm going to say this," Landon said as he stifled a yawn. "But do you think we should have a fire?"

Holly nodded. "I'd like that. It'd be cozier than just lying on the grass. Look at that." She pointed at a wolf who was going in a circle, patting down his own nest. "They flatten the grass for us, and then they flatten it again for themselves." She smiled and softly giggled as the wolf finally settled down.

"He must have a later watch," Landon said. "Good. I hope the wolves and panthers all get a chance to get some sleep."

"Den again, dis is deir time," Hardy said. "De nighttime."

"They are nocturnal beings, true," Vates said. "Though I think everyone's system has been shaken up a bit." Vates looked at the curled-up wolf and sighed. "They must be awfully tired. I'm sure everyone is."

A black bear began to snore.

"And not only from this battle," Vates continued, rubbing his eyes. "Many moons have bloomed and withered since any of us have had a true night's rest in freedom." The flesh beneath Vates's eyes sagged from exhaustion. He smiled wearily at Landon and Holly. "Thank you."

Landon felt guilty about the little sleep he'd had in Grandpa Karl's study the previous night. And for all the sleep he had gotten the past several months. Had he been aware of Volucer Ignis taking over Wonderwood sooner, he probably wouldn't have slept too well, either.

Landon shook his head. "After rescuing the animals from the island, I thought you would all enjoy Wonderwood together as you had before the shadows came and spoiled it. Instead, things got worse."

Vates put his hand on Landon's shoulder. "Sometimes things need to become worse before they can improve. For us, the best is yet to come." Vates looked past Landon and raised an eyebrow. "Ah. . .seems others desired a fire to warm by, as well."

Ditty led the way into camp, carrying a pile of long grass,

which she laid near the center of the circle. A black bear sauntered behind her, and after a word from Ditty, the bear began
scraping around the grass pile with his claw. Soon a dirt ditch
encircled the pile. Ditty's parents, Griggs and Dot, added more
grass to the pile. And Battleroot and some others did the same.

"Too bad we don't have any scrapestone," Hardy mused.
He walked to the grass pile and plopped down before it, as if he
could start a fire by staring at it.

"If I still had my staff, I'd offer it for kindling. Not that it
would help much," Vates said. "So long as Holly allows me to
ride with her, I won't need a staff again." He smiled. "Especially
once we reach Shay Run."

"Vates?" Holly stepped close, leaving Ghost to chew on some
grass. "What happens after Shay Run?"

Vates looked off into the distance, and then he turned his
face to the fading sky. "The Auctor's Kingdom, as Ditty has said.
I'll either be running or on my knees. And then. . ." He continued
gazing upward, his mouth hanging open.

"And then. . ." Landon echoed.

"And then"—Vates lowered his head, beaming—"the great
feast of tea and crumplets!"

Holly made a face. "Crumplets? What are those?"

"I never told you about them?" said Landon.

She shook her head.

Landon looked up, remembering. "I had them at Vates's
house with Hardy and Ditty and Mel—"

Landon closed his eyes, picturing Melech alive and well at
Vates's place. He took a breath and let it out slowly.

"And Melech," he continued. "I think they were part cookie, part biscuit, and part"—he opened one eye at Vates, puckering his face—"don't tell me. Oh yeah, of course. Part crumpet."

They gathered around the pile of grass and Griggs produced a rock. "It's from the cliff," he said. "I was holding it while we were praying, and I was going to use it if all else failed."

"Use it to do what?" Landon asked.

Griggs bowed his head sheepishly. "I was going to throw it at the dragon."

Landon smiled. "Oh." He took it from Griggs and studied it, turning it over. "It's not scrapestone, but maybe it will do."

Landon unsheathed his sword and placed the rock along the blade, pointing downward at the grass. *Shick! Shick!* A few warm-up swipes before—*schiiick!*

A tiny spark landed on the grass. It glowed and then faded.

Landon scraped several more times, producing more sparks, but none of them took. Pausing to catch his breath, he looked around at the eagerly waiting faces. Ditty sat between her parents nearby. It was so good to see them together. Griggs and Dot were nearly as skinny and ragged as they had been on the Island of Arcanum, where they had survived on nothing but runny crab goo. Somehow they looked less wild now in the company of their daughter.

Landon kept staring at them, thinking how much they had been through without ever giving up hope. *They deserve a feast of tea and crumplets—and other goodies,* Landon thought. At least, they deserved it more than he did.

But their quietly watching eyes seemed to say something

else. *We don't deserve anything good; that's why we receive every-thing so humbly.* And Ditty looked the same way, too. Had she ever complained about anything?

"Are you okay, Landon?" Ditty asked. "You're not seeing a giant gold coin flipping in the sky, are you?" She smiled.

Landon blinked. How long had he been staring at her? "Oh! No. Not a gold coin. I was just. . .thinking."

"You know what?" Ditty said, standing. She was holding her book, and she turned to the very back. "We have some empty pages back here. They didn't burn from the dragon's fire, but I wonder if they might for us?"

Before Landon could object, Ditty ripped two sheets from the book and placed them on the grass. She looked at Landon, her big eyes melting him. "Go ahead," she said rapping the book. "The words are all still here."

Landon nodded. Concentrating, he ran the stone down the length of the sword. *Shiiing!* A blue-bright light flew from the blade to the paper, where it glowed green and yellow before bursting into red flame. The party oohed at the flicker of light. Landon set down the stone and poked the burning pages into the grass with his sword. The fire spread throughout the pile, illuminating the oohing and ahhing faces around it.

Landon sat near Ditty. On his other side, Holly and then Vates sat down, sighing and stretching. For a moment it felt like being at summer camp, ready to sing some songs and toast marshmallows before heading back to their cabins. Landon smiled at the thought of walking Ditty to her cabin, taking a detour by the lake along the way. He could sense the closeness of her, her shoulder almost touching his.

The fire was soothing, which Landon thought a little strange considering they had just battled a fire-breathing dragon and escaped his flames. And it was his fire that had destroyed their beautiful forest and homeland. But this fire was different. It *wasn't* his fire. It was their fire. They had collected the grass, and Ditty had contributed two pages from her book, pages that burned freely and gave themselves so the rest of the grass heap could burn. Vates also would have donated his staff, had it not been changed into a serpent at Volucer Ignis's palace and then slurped up by the foul dragon.

Landon's eyelids drooped. He could only imagine how tired everyone else must be. He thought of Bridget and the people and animals with her. He prayed for their safety this night, that they might also find some warmth or shelter. At least Bridget had her bears. They would protect her, Landon knew.

He wondered if Ludo had caught up to the advance party or if the Arcans had caught Ludo before Volucer Ignis fell. As the flames blurred in Landon's fading vision, he saw Ludo running and the Arcans chasing him. Then the Arcans stopped while Ludo kept on running, pushing his way through the tall grass.

But something else happened. A shadow leaked from one of the frozen Arcans, drifting after Ludo through the grass. When Ludo stopped to rest, the shadow kept going, closing the gap. Ludo lay down for the night, and the shadow slipped beneath him.

"Hunh!" Landon gasped. The fire blazed before him. A hand touched his arm. It was Ditty.

"Are you okay, Landon?" she asked. "I thought you fell asleep."

Landon looked at her, firelight dancing in her eyes. "I guess I did. I just saw Ludo, and a shadow chasing after him."

Ditty looked sad but not surprised. "He's never been strong against them."

Something else troubled Landon. "The shadow," he said. "The dragon's still alive, isn't he? Or whatever you call it. I wonder if he can die. How do you kill death?"

"Kill isn't the word," Ditty said softly. "Conquer. Conquer death. And we can't."

Landon squinted. His eyes almost hurt they were so tired. "We can't. But he can."

Ditty nodded. She and Landon spoke his name together: "The Auctor."

Landon noticed movement on his right and looked to see Holly glancing their way. "How will he do it? And when?"

"Soon," Landon said. "I think he'll do it soon." He touched the flat of his sword, thinking, *It's the Auctor's sword.*

"How soon?" asked Holly.

Ditty hugged her knees and leaned forward to look at Holly. "When we take the test."

"Hmm," Holly said. Landon knew she wasn't satisfied; she preferred concrete answers to these abstract ones.

Landon removed all his armor: helmet, breastplate, sword belt, and leg pieces. It felt good to have it off.

"Good night, Holly," he said. "Good night, Ditty." Landon lay on his back, his feet absorbing warmth from the fire. *Tomorrow will be another big day,* he thought. *The Rose of Shay Run.* What would happen there? What would be the Auctor's test?

As Landon dozed, he thought of the man in white looking up from his book. *It's not so much a test as it is all about trust. Will you trust me, Landon Snow? If you do, you will pass the test and see the Auctor's Kingdom.*

Chapter Twelve

Landon's feet were cold. The fire was dead. Others were still sleeping, but Vates was awake. He stood near the wall of grass with Hardy and Ravusmane. Had that wolf slept at all? Did he ever sleep?

With the growing light came the most delicious sound in the world. *Birdsong.* A single bird flitted from grass tip to grass tip, bending each blade and then bouncing into the air. The grass wasn't stiff enough to hold the little bird. The next time the bird flung into the air, it flapped its wings and continued to rise.

"Twee-too!"

Landon sat up. "Epops!"

The little green bird swooped, darting toward Landon before rising again, teasing him.

Landon laughed. "I've missed you. It's good to see you. And good to hear you, too!"

"Twee-too! Twee-too!"

Epops flew in a circle and came down to land on Vates's hand. The old man had glanced up and stretched out his finger for his feathery friend. Then Vates and Hardy resumed their discussion while Ravusmane stood with ears and tail alert and Epops fluffed and preened his feathers.

"Oh," Landon moaned as he stood and stretched. "I'm as stiff as a board!"

Holly was putting her armor on. "Up and add 'em!" she said eagerly.

Landon looked at her. "I didn't think you were such a morning person, Holly."

She was fitting a molded piece of metal over her shin. "If what you said was true about the Arcans being frozen in place—you know, while the dragon sleeps or whatever he's doing—Ungh!" She pulled at a leather strap.

"Yes?" Landon said quizzically. "What do you have in mind? Running them through while they can't move?" This would be bad form if they were worthy foes, but they weren't. They were Arcans. "That's not a bad idea," he muttered to himself.

"Well that, too," Holly said, straightening. "I just want to *count* them. You know." She grinned.

Landon groaned. "Good grief." He shook his head. "We may not have time for that. Bridget will be waiting for us."

"True." Holly gazed in the direction of the still far-off hills. "But I'm a fast counter. All I need to do is count and multiply the columns and rows!"

Ditty was sitting cross-legged, reading her book, pausing now and then to close her eyes and think. She opened her eyes and glanced at Landon, catching him watching her.

"What?" she asked. She smiled from the corner of her mouth.

Landon picked up his helmet and knelt by Ditty on one knee. He felt older than his age, wearing armor and carrying a sword and riding a horse and leading these people and these animals through battle and now toward Shay Run. Yet he still felt like a young boy, too, as if he were playacting these roles.

"This is a big day," Landon said vaguely, "for all of us."

"We're not there yet," said Ditty. She closed her book, looking at it. "But I think you're right." Her fingers caressed the book thoughtfully and deliberately.

"What?" Landon asked, mimicking her earlier question. He wanted to reach over and touch her hair, comb his fingers through it, and pluck out the bits of grass. "Ditty. Are you okay? Is something wrong?"

Her fingers paused, and Ditty sighed and glanced up. Her face had matured since Landon had first met her. Her big eyes still sparkled with cheerfulness, playfulness. But something else was in her expression, too. Something serious and deep.

"Visions and dreams," she said mysteriously. "I think the Auctor has shown me something." She squinted and pursed her lips, seeming to hesitate over something.

"What?" Landon said again. The air felt thick, catching in his throat. It pressed on his chest. "You've seen something. . .good?"

Ditty looked at him and right through him. "We're from two separate worlds, aren't we?" It sounded more like a statement than a question.

Landon swallowed. The air grew thicker. He nodded.

"I've seen this world coming to an end." Ditty closed her eyes, and her eyelids trembled. But she did not cry.

Landon slumped from his knee to sit on the ground. He touched the earth, squeezing dirt and grass between his fingers. It felt so real. It *was* real. Ditty was real. Yet it was another realm from where he'd come from. Would this place really pass away?

Ditty continued. "I've been reading the final chapters in the *Book of Illumination*. It says when the sky turns black and the lowlands lie in waste, the end is near. The evil one will reign another day, and then he'll be destroyed. And then—"

Ditty choked and appeared to break down, but then she regained her composure.

"And then," she continued after taking a deep breath, "the Auctor's Kingdom will reign. There will be a new realm, and this one will be no more."

Landon looked at Ditty, watching as her eyelids fluttered and then calmed.

"Shay Run," Landon said. "You said that's the way to the Auctor's Kingdom."

Ditty breathed deeply, and Landon wondered if she had heard him. Finally she nodded.

"It's in the prophecy. The final test will be the Rose of Shay Run. It will usher in the Auctor's Kingdom."

Landon studied Ditty's face. He lifted his hand, still dirty from the ground, and touched her cheek. Her skin twitched, but she didn't turn away. Landon felt warmth from her skin pass through his entire body. He withdrew his hand and studied his fingers.

"The sky turned black," Landon said, "even though it's now

blue. The valley has been destroyed and lies in waste. Was the dragon destroyed, do you think?"

Ditty shook her head. Although Landon doubted it himself, he was surprised by Ditty's quick response.

"He wasn't? How do you know?"

Ditty's eyelashes lifted. She gazed at the clear sky as if waiting for it to darken again. Then she looked at Landon.

"You know it, too. You sense it because the Auctor brought you here for this purpose." Ditty tapped the book. "It's the final test, Landon. And it will happen at Shay Run. The book—the *Auctor*—says someone will be sent to defeat the dragon at Shay Run. Someone not from this world."

"But. . . ," Landon stammered. "You mean. . ."

Ditty's gaze took hold of him, filling him with fear and boldness, warmth and cold, questions and answers all at once. Then there were just her eyes. Her big, deep, cheerful eyes.

"Yes. You."

All of the emotions Landon had felt earlier came rushing back: when he read the Bible verse in Grandpa Karl's study, when he fell through the trapdoor in the barn, when he and Jalopy flew from the chessboard to the cliff. And he knew—he *knew* it was his destiny to kill the dragon.

"But I can't," he said. "I mean—I tried at the cliff. And then Melech"—he broke off, blinking. "But *how?* How can he be destroyed? I can't do it, Ditty. He's already beyond death. He's too powerful for me."

Ditty nodded, confirming Landon's fears. "I know it. He is too powerful for you. He's more powerful than all of us." She looked around. Others in the camp were milling about, talking or chewing on grass or limbering up for the next leg of their journey. She returned her gaze to Landon. "But the Auctor's given you something, right?" She raised her eyebrows. "He's given you his Word. Hasn't he?"

"Well," Landon said, "yeah, I guess. Back in my world I have a book like that." He pointed to the book in her lap. "My Bible. Which is called the Word sometimes. But I don't have it here, and—"

Landon paused in midthought. He felt his eyebrows rising to match Ditty's as if drawn by an idea.

Ditty tilted her head. "And?"

"Wait a second. His Word. The Auctor's Word." Landon stared, thinking. "My Bible's back in my grandfather's study on the desk. It came originally from Bartholomew G. Benneford—at least he was the first owner of it. And this sword also came from Bart. His initials are scratched right here." Landon pulled it out and turned it to reveal *B.G.B.* etched on the hilt. "The Auctor's Word there. The Auctor sword here. Might that be it? Could this be the Auctor's Word?" Landon twisted the blade and shoved it back into the sheath. "Or doesn't that make any sense at all?"

Instead of shaking her head or smirking at his crazy idea, Ditty opened her eyes wider than ever before.

"What?" Landon said finally. "It's a stretch, huh?"

With her eyes still wide, Ditty lowered her gaze and opened her book. She began flipping pages. Her fingers moved so fast the pages almost seemed to be turning on their own. Landon gaped, imagining his Bible turning pages back on Grandpa Karl's desk *this very moment.* Ditty stopped and gripped the book along either edge.

"Right here," she said. "Listen."

Landon leaned closer, listening.

" 'He shall take the helmet of the kingdom and the sword of the Auctor, which is the Auctor's Word. Also, raise up the shield of faith, which will quench the flames of the evil one.' "

"Whoa," Landon said. "Wow. That sounds incredibly familiar. There's a passage like that in my book, too. Wow."

"Could it be chance?" Ditty said, raising her eyes.

"Mere circumstance?" Landon smiled. "Uh, no. I don't think so. Except one thing I'm not sure about. The shield of faith? What do you think that might be?"

Ditty shrugged. "Hmm. I don't know. But the rest sure seems to fit, doesn't it?"

Landon lifted his helmet, admiring it anew. "The helmet of the kingdom." He patted the sword. "The sword of the Auctor." He looked at Ditty, his smile fading. "There's another verse I read in my book before coming here."

After a moment Ditty glanced down, slowly closed her book, and looked at Landon.

"It said, 'Greater love hath no man than this, that a man lay down his life for his friends.' " Landon paused, waiting for the words to sink in.

"Yes," she said. "That must be true. That is true. He really did love us, didn't he?"

Landon felt a twinge of relief, though he wasn't sure why. "*He*?"

"Melech," Ditty said simply.

"Melech," Landon said, feeling the sound of his friend's

name as he pronounced it. "You think he fulfilled that prophecy?"

Ditty looked hurt, and then her face relaxed. "Well, he did just that. He laid down his life. . .for us."

Landon's twinge of relief flashed to guilt. And then sadness. "I guess I meant, well. . .do you think I'll have to do that, too?" He lowered his head.

Ditty looked older, as if she were a teacher addressing a student. "Would you do that?"

Landon flinched. "Yes. I mean—I already *did*. Or I tried to, anyway. I thought it was my destiny. And yes, I would do it again. I will, I mean, if I have to." He bit his tongue to keep from rambling further.

"It's been fulfilled by Melech," Ditty said. "Maybe that was his part. Maybe you're not supposed to die. . .here." Her eyes flickered and filled with grief over the end of her world.

"What do you think will happen. . .to you?" Landon swallowed a lump in his throat. "To all of us?"

"If we trust the Auctor and stand firm until the end, we'll get to see his Kingdom."

"The new Kingdom?"

"Yes."

Landon and Ditty looked at each other a long time. Landon said, "I'm really glad I got to know you. Whatever happens here— and at Shay Run—I'll never forget you."

Ditty crinkled her eyes, and she leaned over and tapped Landon on the nose. Tap tap. "I hope not," she said. "And thank you."

The ground shivered as Holly's white horse rambled over.

Landon and Ditty looked up.

"Are you two about ready?" Holly asked, beaming down at them. "The natives are getting restless." Behind her sat Vates with Epops perched on his shoulder.

The green bird tilted his head. "Twee-too!"

"All right," said Landon somewhat reluctantly. He stood and helped Ditty up. Looking at her, he said, "We're as ready as we'll ever be, I suppose. Ditty—"

Hardy ambled into view. He looked much better after a night's rest. Putting one hand on each of their shoulders, Hardy glanced at Landon and Ditty.

"How about you two ride togedder on de horsy, hey? I'm fit to trundle de grass today." Hardy grinned, showing off his crooked teeth as his eyes darted back and forth between them.

Landon's face flushed. And his heart leaped a little. He looked at Ditty. "Well?"

"Sure." She smiled, although there was a hint of sadness in her eyes. They could only put off saying good-bye for so long. "Sure, I'd be glad to travel by horseback today."

Jalopy finished jawing a mouthful of dry grass while Landon mounted and helped Ditty up behind him. She took hold of his waist, and it tickled, but not enough to make him laugh. He got used to it, and they trotted off through the grass, leading the way toward the hills.

Landon and Ditty didn't talk as they rode Jalopy through the tall grass. Landon enjoyed Ditty's presence and her touch on his waist, and he silently thanked Hardy a number of times as they trotted along. Landon listened to the swish of the grass and watched the roving lines of ripples where invisible creatures made their paths. The funniest sight was Hardy and Wagglewhip popping up like prairie dogs to check their bearings. Holly and Vates were into another discussion.

The party was able to move more quickly, and the hills in the distance grew larger. Landon noted riffles of grass along either side of him as wolves and panthers tromped by. In the middle distance, the grass appeared to rise still higher. It wasn't until they were practically upon it that they discovered it wasn't grass. It was a frozen army of Arcan soldiers.

Chapter Thirteen

itty finally spoke, stating the obvious. "This is where they stopped."

Although Landon had expected to come across them eventually, the actual sight of rows and rows of motionless figures in grotesque armor, wielding dark, curved blades in midair, and spiked by the skulls of animals was unnerving to say the least.

"They sure did," Landon said quietly as if the Arcan ears were still alert.

Jalopy slowed, and they came right up to the rear flank. Landon wrinkled his nose. "Ugh. They still stink. I'd already forgotten the smell."

Holly and Vates joined them as bears—carrying Griggs and Dot, among others—and panthers and wolves, and then Hardy and Wagglewhip stopped abruptly behind the Arcan line.

Ghost reared, and Holly settled him. "Easy," she said patting the pale horse's neck. "Whoa. They're not attacking.

They're just. . .waiting."

The air above the Arcans wavered like steaming pavement on a summer day. It had taken Landon a moment to notice it. It seemed to waver and then clear, waver and then clear again.

"Do you see that?" he asked, pointing over the skull-topped heads. "The air is moving. Shimmering sort of."

A soft bark drew Landon's attention downward. Ravusmane peered up at him from the grass.

"The shadows are growing restless. I can smell them." He bared his teeth and growled for effect.

"How can you smell anything over. . .*that*?" Landon pinched his nose. "It's disgusting."

"That is what I smell," said Ravusmane. "They stink worse when they're stirring. I fear the dragon may soon be on the rise."

Landon reined Jalopy to the right, pulling gently on her mane. They half galloped along the row of Arcans some distance before turning back and returning to the group. Landon wasn't sure what he was doing. He needed to feel some wind and fresh air to clear his head so he could think. He reined Jalopy in, facing Holly and Vates.

"Can we kill some while they're like this?" Landon asked Vates, searching the old man's face.

Vates furrowed his brow. "Not likely," he said. "As we've seen before, they only crop up in greater numbers. Moreover I doubt they have any substance to impair at this point." The old man looked at Hardy, who stood in a flattened spot between two bears. "What do you think, my friend?"

Hardy drew his sword and jumped straight up, turning in the air while shouting a battle cry. "Ayeee!" His sword sliced the nearest Arcan's neck and came right back around. Somehow, Hardy landed on his feet, panting.

The Arcan's head bobbled like a spring-loaded doll, its horned helmet jiggling.

Holly gasped, while Landon could only stare in astonished silence.

"Nothing but air?" Vates offered.

Hardy turned to face him, his teeth jutting in a snarl. "Nudding but gooey shadow." He grimaced at his sword as if blood might be dripping from it. The blade was clean.

Landon looked at Vates. "Why is that? What's going on?"

"They have no single form, as you have already witnessed. Shadow to flesh and back again. And something like this state that's sort of in-between. If you've noticed, the grass was not crushed from their passing."

Landon looked at the lightly swaying meadow and then at the thousands of densely armored Arcans. A normal army would have left a wide flat trail in their wake.

"But they weren't *moving* as shadows, were they? When they left us, they were still flesh. I felt them. They *bled*." He grimaced at the thought of the sticky, sizzling black fluid.

"Their weight is felt only by living creatures," Vates explained. Landon remembered Vates had experienced evil's many forms longer than he had. Probably longer than anyone else here had. "By *truly* living creatures," he added. "The grass parted from their armor, but would not yield to their substance no matter what their form. They simply have no effect on the inanimate or the plant life. Vegetation has no soul to be soiled by darkness."

"Weird," said Holly, eyeing the Arcan horde. "They're like ghosts." She quickly patted her horse. "No offense."

Ghost whinnied in response.

Landon wondered if the formation of Arcans might be toppled like so many dominos, and he nudged Jalopy to draw alongside a soldier. Drawing his sword, Landon poked the Arcan's back, pinging the metallic plate bordered by bone. Landon pushed, but the armor did not move. He then sliced the shadowy neck just to see for himself. His sword plowed slowly through the dark, gaseous space before flying out again. Some substance was there. It was weird.

Turning to face the others, Landon said, "Let's go around and leave them. I've got a feeling they won't stay like this all day."

A sucking, hissing sound answered, as if the entire army was breathing as one.

Ditty tapped Landon's shoulder, and he jumped.

"Sorry," she said close to his ear. "I didn't mean to startle you. I think I saw something moving up there in the ranks. There! It just darted between two Arcans. Did you see it?"

"Ravusmane!" Landon hollered, forgetting the wolf was right there. "Can you run through the ranks, you and the wolves, and check it out? I don't want to be ambushed from behind once we pass these. . .things."

A raspy "Raow" came from his left, where Landon saw a

panther looking at him expectantly.

"Yes, please, by all means go with the wolves. There are a lot of Arcans to inspect."

The wolves and panthers zipped into action, threading the rows and columns of Arcans silently. Landon got dizzy trying to keep track of them bounding and loping this way and that. Eventually, the panthers and wolves all returned, one panther carrying something that was squirming in its mouth. Ravusmane and the panther approached Landon together.

"We have found this stray among them," Ravusmane said, "and he is one of our own."

"It's Feister," Ditty exclaimed, climbing down to calm the frenzied ferret. The panther released him, and Feister latched onto Ditty's hand and climbed to her shoulder. He nuzzled her ear, provoking a giggle, and then made a couple funny squeaks before sniffing the air, turning his head, and leaping a la flying squirrel to the ground, where he dashed off among the Arcans.

"Where is he going?" Landon asked.

Hardy lunged after Feister as if to catch his little tail. "Stop! Rodent!"

Ravusmane watched Feister scamper away and then looked up at Landon. "It's okay. He is only returning to his master."

"What?" said Landon. "Ludo's *here*?" He scanned the ranks again. The air around the Arcans was darkening. So was the sky. Landon didn't like the looks of it.

Ravusmane explained. "Ludo's at the front line. It looks like he was caught by surprise from behind."

"Is he alive? Is he okay?"

Ravusmane nodded, and Landon thought he detected a smirk. "Oh, he is alive. But a bit shook up."

Landon didn't know whether to be annoyed or amused. With a reluctant sigh, he dismounted and put his hands on his hips.

"Will you show me where he is, Ravusmane?"

"Of course."

Ditty said, "Me, too."

"All right," said Landon. "Hardy, will you take Jalopy around that way? We'll meet you out front again. The Arcans are too close together for her to get through."

"Righty ho," said Hardy, eagerly climbing onto the horse.

Before Landon entered the field of Arcans, Holly called to him.

"I'm taking Ghost around the other way, okay? And, Hardy?"

Hardy bowed his head. "Miss Holly?"

"Could you do me a favor and count the columns, starting here." She pointed to the Arcan Landon had poked in the back. "I'll count going this way, and then we can come up with a grand total together."

Hardy raised his head. "I will count dem for you, Miss."

"Thank you."

Landon looked at his sister, and when she smiled happily at him, he rolled his eyes.

Walking among the Arcans was like entering a cornfield of dark, leering scarecrows wielding black sickles. The air grew thick with their stench as black wisps curled and floated from their wraithlike forms. Landon breathed in short gasps, holding each breath as long as he could before snatching another one. There was a moment where he thought he lost Ravusmane and

Ditty both, and he spun wildly, seeing endless rows of his enemy. He was about to cry out when he heard Ditty's voice.

"This way, Landon."

He turned and followed, relieved to have someone to look at other than the Arcans. Ditty was dressed in worker clothes, drab coveralls over a dirty shirt and brown boots. Landon was surprised he hadn't noticed her clothes before. Everyone was dressed the same, more or less, other than him and Holly and Bridget. And everyone was dirty and chalky with grit.

The shadows on the ground began to move, drifting in various directions, which played tricks on Landon's vision and distracted him from where he was going. *Keep after Ditty*, he told himself. *Don't lose her.*

Finally, they reached the end of the rows, which was the front rank, and stepped through into tall grass. It was like coming up from underwater.

"Hunh!" Landon gasped and took several deep breaths, putting his hands on his hips and arching his back. "Whew. That was nasty." Turning to face the army provoked another gasp. It was much different being in front of them, having the Arcans looking your way, than to be standing behind them. With the Arcans' black blades all held high, Landon had to fight the urge to raise his own sword in defense.

"A-hay! A-hip! A-hi and a-hee! Here come a wolf, a girl, and a boy to rescue me!"

Ravusmane stood facing Ludo like a pointer, his nose and legs fixed in position.

"Uncle Ludo!" Ditty exclaimed. "Are you all right?"

Ludo lay facedown in the grass with an Arcan's foot planted firmly in his back. The same Arcan's sword hovered about two feet from Ludo's neck. Landon approached warily, eyeing the agitated shadows swarming Ludo's body.

"Don't get too close, Ditty," Landon warned. "I've seen what happens when the shadows sneak up on you."

"I have, too," Ditty said sadly. She looked at Landon. "I was there, you know."

Landon sighed apologetically. "Of course." He had to be careful about the shadows getting to him, as they had tried to in the past. They could darken one's mind and fill it with doubts and evil thoughts. Landon shook his head to keep it clear. "Okay. Stand back."

Ditty stepped aside for Landon, as he unsheathed his sword and held it just below the Arcan's knee, or where the knee should be. "Ready?" Landon asked Ludo, who was craning his neck to look up at him. Ludo nodded nervously.

"Ready! Please miss my heady!"

The Arcan's face slightly swelled and then hissed. Shadows slid from the Arcan's foot right into his armor, rippling upward. Before Landon could slice or chop, the Arcan's shin guard and foot flap clinked together onto Ludo's back.

The scrawny man buried his face in the grass. "Ack and alack! I'm under attack!"

Landon slowly withdrew his sword, keeping it at the ready. The Arcan remained standing on one leg, leaning onto nothing, defying gravity. More than anything, the remaining shadows on the ground concerned Landon. He knew Ludo couldn't be trusted.

Especially when he was under the shadows' influence. How long had he been lying here amid the shadows?

Ludo looked up. "I'm okay?" He tipped his head sideways as if checking to see it was still attached. "Hip hip hooray!"

Landon nudged Ludo with his foot, still keeping his sword at the ready.

Something sprang from under Ludo's armpit, and Landon jumped, raising his sword. The ferret raced excitedly back and forth in a horseshoe around its master's head.

"Feister!" Landon said. "Don't do that!"

Glancing at Landon's raised sword, Ludo arched his orange eyebrows, puckering his mouth beneath his pointed nose. "I know what you might suspect. But my brain they did not infect!"

"How could you withstand them?" Landon asked. "When before they influenced you so easily?"

"Aha!" said Ludo pushing up like an inchworm. "Aha! I found this or did it find me? It tripped up Ludo and stopped the army!" As he rose to his knees he held up a brilliant shield, which reflected more light than seemed possible from the increasingly hazy sky.

Ditty gasped. "The shield of faith. Ludo. . .Landon. . .that's it."

The shield had two points at the top and one at the bottom. On its face was etched a beautiful rose.

"The Rose of Shay Run," Landon whispered. He could hardly believe it. Without thinking, he touched the shield gently with his sword. A remarkable thing happened. The rose's stem climbed onto the sword, beginning at the tip and running up to the hilt. Landon almost let go. But he held on, trembling.

"And look!" Ditty exclaimed, pointing at the shield. The rose had bloomed broader, bordered by a splayed leaf. Meanwhile its stem appeared only on Landon's sword, having vanished from the shield.

"Amazing," Landon breathed. "Utterly amazing."

Ravusmane moved from his pointer position, sniffing Ludo, who giggled, and Feister, who squeaked, and then passing his nose over the shield and the sword.

"It carries the Rose's scent." The wolf raised his muzzle and turned, following it until he faced the hills.

Landon felt his arms lifting, the stem-etched blade drawing them upward. He, too, swiveled to face the hills. "We're definitely being directed that way."

From one direction galloped Ghost with Holly and Vates riding. From the other direction, Jalopy reared up, whinnying, and Hardy hollered, "Heighty ho!" from her back.

Soon the wolves, panthers, bears, and the others on foot were gathered out in front of the Arcan army. Hardy dismounted Jalopy and returned her to Landon.

"She's a good horsy," Hardy said, patting her neck. "Not Melech," he added, dropping his voice. "But dere's never going to be anudder like him."

Landon nodded solemnly before mounting and helping Ditty up. He let Ludo carry the shield, a move that made the little man beam and hop with glee. In fact, Ludo and Feister were already skipping ahead of the pack in the direction of the hills. Ludo sang, "A skip diddly dee! The shield protected me!

A dip diddly doo! Landon Snow is noble and true!"

Landon laughed when he heard him. It might not be true, but it was certainly nice to hear.

Chapter Fourteen

The party moved through the grasses. Loping, trotting, padding invisibly beneath rippling wakes. Landon kept looking at his sword. The fine lines of the rose stem swayed slightly in a wave from tip to hilt. Tiny leaves sprouted along it. Or were they thorns?

"It's getting darker back there." Ditty's voice came at his shoulder. "Like a big storm is about to chase us."

"That's an effective way to put it," said Landon. "Did you hear what the total count was for the Arcans?"

Holly and Hardy had met and shared their numbers. And Holly had put them together along with the column number from the side and come up with a total for the army.

"A thousand and something? I forget what she said."

"A big number, anyway," Landon said. "I'm really glad they didn't kill Ludo." The shield bearer continued his happy skipping and singing, although Landon could no longer make out the words.

"Do you think it was the fall of Volucer Ignis that stopped them, or the shield of faith?"

Landon tilted his head. "I hadn't thought of that. They were stopped right there, weren't they. Do you think the advance group might have dropped it on purpose?"

"Or maybe they didn't do it on purpose, but it was part of the Auctor's purpose?"

Landon squinted. Ludo was getting farther ahead. With a kick to Jalopy's flank, Landon shifted the horse to a higher gear. "Hyah!"

"Where are we going?" asked Ditty, tightening her squeeze on Landon's waist.

"I want that shield *behind* us, not in front of us," Landon explained. "If it did stop that entire army, then we need it back there." He glanced over his shoulder. The air wasn't only getting darker; it was moving. A breeze kicked up. "We need it back there *now*."

"Ludo!" Landon hollered. "Stop! Drop back! Drop back!"

Ditty joined in, shouting. They finally caught Ludo and cut him off. With his next singing skip, Ludo bounced right into Jalopy and fell backward in the grass.

Smiling up at them, Ludo waved the shield. "This rose is so light I could fly! It wants to carry me right to the sky!"

Landon shook his head wondering if Ludo had gone mad. It wouldn't be the first time. At least it was a good sort of crazy this time and not a shadowy evil.

"We need you in the back, Ludo, not the front. The shield will protect us."

"But it wants to go for'd! It pulls at the hills like your sword!"

"Well," said Landon looking back, "just wait here then until the others catch up. Okay?"

Ludo grinned. "Okay. Okay. I'll do as you say. But don't blame me for the shield's velocity!" As he waved the shield, Landon noticed the rose had turned pink. He looked at his sword. The stem was turning green.

Meanwhile the rising wall of darkness was bearing down on them like a tidal wave.

Landon raised his sword and circled it over his head. "Hurry, everybody! Come on!"

Holly and Vates zipped past and then wheeled about. "Holy thunderstorm, Landon," said Holly. "It's coming fast."

Vates lifted his hand and eyed the sky as if feeling for something. "Except it isn't holy," he added. "And I'm afraid it carries more than thunder."

Landon glanced at the old man. "Do you think Volucer Ignis is on the move?"

Vates turned and studied him. The swelling wind whipped Vates's hair behind him. The lines across Vates's face stiffened. Slowly, he nodded.

When Landon was sure everyone had run safely past them, he commanded Ludo to his feet. The gust almost blew the little man over.

"Make sure you stay behind everyone. Okay, Ludo?" The wind ripped his words away.

"Okay?" he repeated.

Ludo bowed, bending like a reed against the wind. He nodded with his whole body, surfing the wind with the shield clasped against his chest.

"Good!" Landon hollered. It was getting useless trying to shout over the wind. He looked to the sky, alarmed at the black streaks reaching overhead like fingers. Where was Epops? He could sure use an air report. And it was always nice just having that little green bird around. There was something comforting about his presence. *Could Epops even fight his way back to us through this blustery weather?* Landon wondered.

His distinct birdsong seemed to come from high above, so Landon was startled when Epops swooped quickly into view.

"Twee-*too*!"

Epops flew to Vates and lit on his shoulder after three landing attempts, blowing sideways. His green plumage had never been so ruffled.

Ghost sauntered over, his head bowed low. Vates had his ear to the bird while he chirped and sang. Vates then leaned to Holly's ear, and Holly in turn gave Landon the update on Bridget and her party.

"Busy!" is all Landon heard, although he saw Holly's mouth move more than that.

"What?" He cupped his ear, which caused the wind to howl even louder. Landon shook his head. "Busy?"

Ghost and Jalopy pressed alongside each other so brother and sister could talk.

"I said Bridget and the people have been busy. They're

peeling petals from a giant rose and plucking leaves and making something."

Epops tweeted. Vates nodded and leaned in, his gray hair flying in Landon's face.

"They're making boats of the leaves and sails from the petals. And"—he listened as Epops sang more notes—"stitching the sails to the leaf-boats with some sticky thread. Spider-web thread."

Epops opened his wings and launched a few feet away, where he flapped vigorously to return to Vates's shoulder. Landon was shaking his head, wondering if he'd been hearing everything correctly.

"Leaf boats?" He studied Vates, searching the old man's eyes between waves of flying gray hair. "Why?" he shouted. He wanted to ask, *Why on earth are they making boats and sails?* And should they be dismantling the Rose at all? It was too much to get out through the wind.

Epops hunkered down on Vates's shoulder. The bird appeared to be squinting; his feathers riffling across his tiny black eyes. He cocked his head toward Holly and then swiveled to look at Landon. "Too-twee!"

Landon blinked, staring. "Really?" he said, squinting at the little green bird. "She did?"

"Too-*twee*. *Twee*-too!"

Holly was fighting her own flying hair, pulling strands from her mouth and pushing them from her eyes. Her eyes glinted at Landon. "You understood that?" She turned toward the bird and then turned back after catching a mouthful of Vates's hair.

Landon wanted to laugh. "Our little sister had a vision. They're making not only *leaf* boats, but *life* boats." Another thought hit him. "Vates? Is there *water* up there?" By *up there*, he meant in the hills.

Vates's squint grew tighter. Either his eyes were watering from the wind, or he was reacting emotionally to their conversation. It wasn't he who answered Landon, but Ditty.

"According to the book," she yelled, "there's a river near the Rose that flows from the highest mountain and falls into the sea. That is Shay Run."

Holly shouted, "Falls?"

Ditty nodded. "Waterfall."

A yelp sounded. Ludo was leaning at a forty-five degree angle into the wind, holding the shield against it, grimacing. "Are you going to soon run?" he screamed. "Because this isn't too fun!"

"Let's go," said Landon without a moment's hesitation. "Hold on," he said to Ditty as he wheeled Jalopy about. They swung a loop around Ludo, making sure no stragglers had fallen behind, and then galloped toward the hills. With the wind at their backs, they quickly caught the rest of the pack. Landon was glad to see the bears carrying Dot and Griggs out front, blazing a path through the tall grass, and the others following behind, not having to fight their way through. After a while, the bears dropped back and another riderless bear and two panthers became the vanguard. They were leaving an unmistakable trail—*like parting the Red Sea*, Landon thought—but it's not like they were trying to hide it as Bridget's company had done so well. They were in too much of a hurry for that now. *Besides,* Landon thought, *if Volucer Ignis was soon on the move, he wouldn't be looking for trails in the grass.* Landon had the strange feeling the dragon would know just where to search for them.

The hills grew larger in the middle distance, yet they didn't seem to be getting much closer—partly because the shadowy air from behind was dimming the view ahead, too. What had Ditty said? Landon felt her hands on his waist, his own fingers clutching Jalopy's coarse mane. *A river flows from the highest mountain.* Highest mountain? A mountain? He had only seen hills up ahead. Was that the outline of a mountain behind the hills? He squinted, wishing he had the brass telescope he'd had onboard ship when they sailed to the Island of Arcanum. But the shape behind the hills appeared to be mist or sky or nothing.

Jalopy's gallop rhythm got into Landon. *Dubba-bump, dubba-bump, dubba-bump.* Landon's sword beat gently along his hip. His breastplate and leg pieces jounced slightly, catching wafts of wind beneath each lift. *Dubba-bump, dubba-bump.*

The highest mountain. Landon kept looking for it as if it were a huge ship ready to break through the fog. How come he couldn't see it?

When the realization struck him, it was like a flashback of all his adventures in this other realm rolled into one overlapping image. The mountain was the mist and the sky beyond the hills—it was so massive he couldn't see where it ended to either side, or where the top even began to taper. It made the wall Volucer Ignis had been forcing the people to construct in the valley seem as small as a ripple in the sand. Once Landon realized the mountain was there, that he had in fact been seeing it all along, everything took on a new color. A giant rose seemed only fitting. The hills were flower mounds at the base of the Auctor's mountain.

"Aye-yee! Aye-yee! Aye-yee!"

Ludo was skipping joyfully despite the blustering black mass swelling behind him. With each of Ludo's flying leaps, the wind thrust him several extra feet so that he seemed to defy gravity. Flouncing behind Ludo's neck like a ponytail was his ferret, Feister, clinging to Ludo's back collar with only his forepaws. In distinct contrast to his master's grinning glee, the poor rodent looked frightened to death.

Just when the hills began to loom near, the group's view became obscured by a copse of evergreens. The bears, wolves, and panthers growled and howled and meowed their pleasure at entering the wood. Landon was also glad to be among the towering green firs and in from the open prairie. It smelled of Christmas, and the thick-needled boughs whooshed and sighed in greeting. No sooner had they expressed their welcome, however, than the same branches began to whine and moan in warning. Through the wonderful smell of pine, Landon caught a whiff of smoke riding the breeze behind them.

Following the hint of smoke came a faint rumbling. The Arcan army was on the march. The wind began to die, only amplifying the rhythmic *thrum* of thousands of armored feet. *They have weight again,* Landon thought. But then he realized he wasn't *feeling* their movement so much as *hearing* it. A distant *rhum. Rhum. Rhum.* The more he listened, however, the more he could begin to feel it. *Rhum. Rhum. Rhum.* The sound was beating into him.

Ditty's hands tightened on his waist. Her voice came as sweet relief to his ears. "We're almost there. Look at your sword."

Landon looked. The stalk and leaves were fully green, almost glowing up and down the silver blade. Brown thorns had also budded, bare and barbed. Whoever received the sword's next sting would feel more than one point, Landon guessed. And he wondered if it might prove hard to draw the sword back out again. Lightly tracing the green stem, he grazed his finger across a thorn, feeling only smooth steel. When he lifted his finger, however, there was a red dot of blood.

When he showed Ditty his fingertip, her eyes widened.

The hill's rise took them by surprise. After the flat, needle-covered soil of the wood, they suddenly found themselves scrambling uphill. The trees climbed with them, providing cover and comforting sighs over the distant drumming clang of Arcan armor. Landon kept looking at his sword and his finger, awed. He wanted Ludo nearby—or rather he wanted the shield at hand. Where had Ludo gone to with the shield?

A gray wolf bounded their way. It was Ravusmane.

"As the stench of smoke billows from behind, so the scent of Rose summons us ahead. Do you smell it?"

Landon forgot Ludo for the moment and closed his eyes. Filtering through the pine and smoke, he searched for the scent. "Yes!" he said opening his eyes. "We must be—"

There. Rising from the hill in a clearing of evergreens was a stalk like the one fabled Jack must have climbed to find his giant. This stalk bore leaves and thorns—*like on my sword*—and was topped by a magnificent flower, bigger and more beautiful than Landon had even imagined.

Everyone stepped into the clearing in rapt silence. Even the breeze seemed to still in its presence. Landon felt he could have stared up at it, soaking in its fragrance forever.

Finally, Holly spoke. "It's a tower flower. A flower tower. It's *huge*. Landon—"

"I know. I can see. And *smell*. It's awesome."

"But Landon, where is Bridget? And where are all the others?"

Landon blinked, returning to reality. Where were Ludo and the shield, for that matter? He was about to consult Ravusmane or Epops for help, when an ear-piercing shriek came from high overhead.

Chapter Fifteen

First things first. Landon panicked.

"Bridget! Ludo! Ravusmane! Epops!" He spun Jalopy in a circle, hollering.

Ditty gripped his shoulders. "Landon. This is it. Now's the time. . .*to trust*."

Were there shadows flying among the trees, or was he imagining them? She was right, of course. They were here. They had reached the Rose of Shay Run. And here's where the test would occur. Was it as simple a matter as trust? Landon stared at the darkening sky, anticipating another bloodcurdling cry. His heart pounded. The blackness swirled. Was it about to form a tornado of shadows and smoke? Would the Rose be swept up and hurled away? Would all hope be lost? Was this test for everyone? Or only for him?

Landon had a flashback of images in an instant. But then he was left with one picture. It was of himself in his grandfather's study. He'd just heard his grandfather cry outside. There'd been an accident. Landon had wondered if life itself might be an accident, and that's when the pages in his Bible had begun to turn. Now the pages were turning again. He could sense it. He could feel it. He could see it. The pages were turning, which meant the Auctor was stirring. He wanted to tell Landon something.

What is it? Landon wondered. He wasn't aware whether he was speaking his thoughts aloud. *What is it you want to tell me? I can't see the pages.*

The reddish pink petals of the Rose turned white. One of them fell. And then another, and another. On their way down, they caught on the thorns, tearing. And bleeding. The petals were stained red by the time they reached the ground. They sank into the earth, being swallowed up. A while later, they came out on a river that carried them swiftly away. The river appeared to end, flowing straight into the sky. But it was a waterfall. The water gushed over, throwing white petals into the air. The blood had been rinsed clean. The petals did not fall. They floated and gathered in the air, growing bigger and brighter than ever. Landon thought he was seeing a brilliant butterfly spreading its wings. But it was not a butterfly. It was a man. It was the man in white, opening wide his arms.

"Greater love hath no man than this, that a man lay down his life for his friends."

"That's what I did for you, Landon Snow. Those who believe in me are my friends. I have laid down my life for you all."

The rose above was reddish pink. So beautiful was its blossom that Landon hadn't noticed the lifeboat-sized leaves or jagged thorns. The vision had occurred in an instant, a second after Ditty had said the word *trust*.

"I trust him," Landon said to Ditty. "The Auctor's been watching over us all along. And he came himself, like us, to save us. The victory's already won, if we believe in him."

Ditty's eyes watered. Landon sat half turned, looking at her. He wanted to look into her big shining eyes for a long time, relishing their shared faith. He could even see the Rose reflected in her eyes. Sitting on horseback beneath the flower gazing into Ditty's eyes and knowing the Auctor was real; Landon breathed it all in. And then an orange streak lit up the sky.

Landon saw that reflected in Ditty's eyes, as well. She looked up, and then he did, too. Had someone screamed? Landon glanced around. Everyone was gazing at the sky with their mouths open, waiting for another firework. The scream came from the air. It wasn't the dragon. It was the boy Max, who was *riding* the dragon.

"We're back!" Max stretched the word *back* into another shriek. "And there's nowhere to hide!" He laughed wickedly.

Nowhere to hide? This seemed a weak threat as Landon and the rest of the group were surrounded by evergreens and partially covered by the giant Rose. A moment later, however, the threat took on some force.

Throoooosh!

A plume of orange flame shot from the sky, igniting a nearby tree. Heat blasted all the way to the ground. It felt like opening the door to a furnace. Landon shielded his face with his left arm and instinctively raised his sword with his right. When he uncovered his eyes, the tree was a charred, smoking telephone pole with a few spindly twigs for branches.

"It's not safe here," Ditty said. She sounded surprised, mystified even. Wasn't the Rose supposed to protect them? Was this the test of faith? That they stand here while Volucer Ignis burned everything around them? "Landon," she pleaded, "what should we do?"

Landon first thought of Bridget and her company. Where were they? And then he remembered the shield bearing the emblem of the Rose. Where was Ludo? Holly and Vates came over on Ghost. Hardy, Wagglewhip, Ravusmane, Griggs, Dot, and a few bears and panthers also approached. They were murmuring, wondering about their next move.

Landon felt confident the Auctor had a plan; he only wished he knew what it was! Telling everyone about the rose-petal vision he'd just had probably wouldn't console them much in the moment. Bridget had a vision and was busy making leaf boats.

Vates climbed down from Ghost and stretched his back, grimacing. When he looked at Landon, he was actually smiling. The old man's face glowed red as another evergreen burst into flame across the clearing.

Vates spread his arms as if he were standing in a garden enjoying a sunny day. "I didn't know if I'd ever make it here. Now we're here. The prophecy is true, of course." He gazed up not at the smoke-filled sky but at the giant flower. "The Rose of Shay Run. It is gorgeous." He lowered his gaze to Landon. "Thank you."

Landon tilted his head. "For what?"

"For listening and seeing. For responding to the Auctor. For believing even when things might not have seemed to make sense."

Landon decided to share his vision, or at least the significance of it, briefly.

"The Auctor himself once came here," he said, realizing the truth of it even more deeply as he spoke. "He came *here*." It was true. This was the place where he had come, down from the highest mountain. "Like the river," Landon added. "And he is still present here"—Landon glanced at the Rose—"and will lead us to his Kingdom. If we believe."

Vates's smiled broadened.

Hardy raised his hand, his stocky arm sticking up like he had a question. "I do believe! But I also believe de trees are poofing and de dragon is just getting warmed up!"

Others nodded and murmured. Beyond the roaring crackle of fire came a rhythmic crunching. The army of Arcans had reached the hill.

Landon looked at Ravusmane. "Do you know where the river is? Can you tell by the air?" Landon lifted his nose, sniffing.

Ravusmane raised his snout, but it was his ears that seemed to be working. His ears twitched in and out, and then left and right until his whole body turned to the right. "The river lies in that direction." He angled his head and sniffed. "Our friends are waiting there for us."

Despite the fiery mayhem erupting around him, Landon was reluctant to leave the Rose. "Can you tell where Ludo is? Do you know his scent, Ravusmane?"

The wolf swiveled the other direction. "I think I see him now."

"Aye-yip! Aye-*ow!* Aye-yee! They're coming after me!"

Ludo bounded into the clearing holding the shield out-stretched before him. Feister was draped over Ludo's shoulder, facing backward. The rattling crunch of Arcans grew behind them.

"What happened?" Ditty asked. "Where did you go, Uncle Ludo?"

Ludo paused, panting. "The trees." He waved his hand, gesturing vaguely at the evergreens. "They do so please." He looked at Landon with quivering lip and pitiably sad blue eyes. "I miss my home. I no longer want to roam." He dropped the shield and bent over, wheezing.

Landon felt a tug at his heart. He remembered Ludo's towering Whump Tree well. So much had happened around it and inside it.

"Well, we're done roaming, Ludo," Landon said. "Almost, anyway. Let's go, everyone. To the river!"

Landon hopped down to retrieve the shield. It felt good in his hand. *Come on, Volucer Ignis,* he thought. *Try blasting through this.*

A funnel of fire shot from the sky, disintegrating what was left of an already burnt tree. The blaze of heat propelled everyone into motion over the clearing and down into the wood on the other side. Landon looked up to see the shadowy form of the dragon flying off through the smoke. He reconsidered his challenge regarding the shield and tucked it close, jogging past the giant stem of the Rose. "Take Jalopy," he told Ditty, who then rode off over the clearing. Hardy and Wagglewhip helped Ludo, who kept looking at the evergreens, or what was left of them, weeping. At the clearing's edge, Landon paused and looked back.

Vates was taking his time, moving his limbs slowly. Strangely, he seemed to be enjoying this, as if the fire or heat couldn't touch him. Maybe they couldn't.

Holly was riding Ghost around the stalk, gazing upward. *She couldn't be,* Landon thought. "Come on, Holly!" he shouted. "Get out of there!"

Holly looked at Landon, glanced back up at the Rose, and then trotted Ghost over.

"You were not counting petals," Landon said dryly.

Holly laughed. "Of course not! I was counting leaves and thorns. Did you notice how green the leaves are? They look newer than the stem."

Landon looked. The leaves did appear fresh. Then again, so did the petals.

Holly reined Ghost, half turning. "I would've counted the petals if I could see them." She grinned and swung Ghost away, trotting down the hill.

Vates was the only one left. He continued his leisurely garden walk. A fireball burst behind him, turning him into a dark silhouette against a circle of yellow light. The blaze settled, and Vates kept walking.

Landon raced out to the old man. "Do you want to use this as a cane?" He offered him his sword.

Vates looked at it. "Those leaves do look new, don't they?"

It was true. The leaves on the sword also appeared brighter than the wavy stem. Landon flipped over the shield and connected the Rose emblem to the sword's stem. Vates gasped and then sighed.

"Almost as pretty as the real thing." He closed his eyes, inhaling the Rose's fragrance.

"Don't you think we should hurry, Vates?"

The prophet's smile refused to fade. Though his skin was completely weathered and his long hair feathery thin, his eyes—those sparkling eyes—seemed to have grown younger, if that was possible. Erase the rest of his face, and Landon could imagine he was looking into the eyes of a young man or even a boy.

The air rumbled. The clatter of metal-and-bone armor beat against Landon's ears as the first wave of Arcans emerged across the hill. The burning trunks of trees made a fitting frame for the skull-topped warriors. They were advancing quickly, steadily, breaking rank around the massive Rose stem and closing rank again on this side.

With his shield and sword Landon knew he could take on as many Arcans as attacked him. But Vates could barely move, let alone defend himself. And Landon wasn't sure how long he could hold the enemy off both of them.

Vates closed his glistening eyes.

That's right, Landon thought. *He can pray. He can always pray.* Landon was looking at the bravest prayer warrior this realm had ever seen. Landon was about to step around Vates to cover his back, when, with his eyes still pressed shut, the old man smiled.

"I know what you're thinking," he said to Landon. "*The old man's given up. He's finally giving in to the evil one.*"

Landon shook his head. "Oh, no. I thought you were praying."

Vates nodded, raising his eyebrows and still smiling. "Oh, that I am. I try to always pray in one way or another. What I'm praying for particularly now is that Epops delivered my message in time to your sister."

Landon frowned. "You were riding Ghost with Holly. Why didn't you tell her yourself?" The Arcans were thirty feet away. March, march, march. . .

"Not Holly. Bridget. The message was for Bridget. Now let's see if my prayer has been answered."

Landon stood battle ready, his feet shoulder-width apart, his shield at an angle across his chest, and his sword out front, tight in his hand, yet loose in his arm. The Arcans raised their curved black blades as one, like an extremely wide thresher about to harvest corn. Were they going to slow their cadence? Or did they plan to merely mow him down and continue without breaking their monotonous stride?

They have another thing coming if that's what they plan to do, Landon thought. No way were they were going to all get past him.

Something moved behind him. Vates. Landon glanced over his shoulder to see Vates stepping shakily into the woods. Landon backed up with him, hollering. "What are you doing now, Vates? It's a little late to run." Landon's sword arm tensed. The phalanx was only ten feet away!

"Aha!" Vates laughed. "Oh, and it is marvelous. Better than I'd expected."

With the advancing Arcans about to strike, Landon raised his shield and saw a remarkable sight reflected on the back of it.

As the first Arcan blade clanged across the front of the shield, Landon watched Vates climb into an enormous leaf.

Clang!

Clank!

Landon warded off two more blows and then thrust his shield arm wide to follow it with a slash of his sword.

"I'll need a push, I'm afraid!" Vates hollered. "I hadn't thought of that. Thank the Auctor you're still here!"

Shoving two more Arcans aside and stabbing a third, Landon turned and ran to Vates. There was no time to think, only to push.

Sheathing his sword and dangling the shield over the lip of the giant leaf, Landon leaned into it and pushed. The leaf was rigid as fiberglass and cupped, pointed in the front and back and sloped to the keel-stem along the bottom. It lay at an angle in the dirt since the bottom wasn't flat. Grunting, Landon felt the leaf shift free, and then he was running full out behind it, struggling to hang on as they careered downhill. He felt like a bobsledder on the loose.

"Whee-hee-hee!" Vates was laughing like a child, gripping the sides of the leaf as it shifted to and fro. There was no way to steer other than by leaning, so as trees zoomed at them, Landon leaned hard in either direction to avoid them. Vates just kept laughing, having the time of his life.

They raced up a small ridge, caught some air, and then continued sliding down the hill. The river appeared below.

"That's right!" Vates exclaimed after they'd bumped back to earth after the jump. "The petal-sail! I almost forgot."

Landon was too busy looking for trees to engage in conversation. In the back of his mind, however, he wondered, *Petal-sail?*

Vates bent over in the leaf-boat. Bent over, he slid back till he bumped Landon's shield. He was murmuring into the boat's bottom before sitting back up, raising two sets of sticks on either side. Across the sticks spanned a saggy red quilt, which blocked Landon's view as it rose from inside the leaf.

"Look out!" Landon yelled. But Vates couldn't hear him. The moment Landon opened his mouth the saggy quilt snapped up and back, billowing into a parachute. And then Landon's feet left the ground.

He guessed they must have hit another ridge, although he hadn't seen one coming. Then he realized it was the parachute that had lifted them. The *petal-sail.* Hanging on with all his strength, he looked down to see water. They were over the river, gently descending toward the racing water.

Chapter Sixteen

Splash!

Landon gasped as the biting cold took hold of him. No sooner had they hit the water than they were being towed toward shore. The water flowed by quickly, and Landon took in a couple gulps as he caught his breath. Once he tasted it, he wanted more. It was the purest, sweetest, most refreshing water he'd ever drunk. And he was thirsty.

Hundreds of people and animals lined the shore. With the water rushing past his ears, it was hard to hear, but Landon thought they were cheering. A few stocky men were pulling in the rope that towed the leaf-boat. Either Vates had thrown out a line to someone as they sailed overhead, or someone from shore had a really good throwing arm.

Upstream, Landon noticed a remarkable sight. Hundreds of similar leaf-boats were in the water, bumping together and kept from floating downstream by a vast net. Bridget and her crew had been astoundingly productive making so many boats!

Landon clambered ashore with help from dozens of hands as another cheer rose up. "The first shall be last," someone shouted, to which the crowd responded, "And the last shall be first!" Vates remained seated in the leaf-boat.

Giggling, the old man smiled at Landon. "I guess we were the last ones here."

Landon looked around at the crowd of animals and people, the shimmering river, the collection of leaf-boats waiting behind the net. It was bewildering. Even the strip of sky mirroring the river was blue. Only faint wisps of smoke clouded it. The trees along the riverbank were not evergreens but big, spread-limbed, leafy affairs. With the cheers and hubbub of the crowd, had everyone forgotten the Arcans and the dragon? Even Landon was starting to forget them as if they were part of a dark dream long ago.

"Landon! Landon!"

Bridget bustled her way through the crowd and then burst out, her arms reaching for her brother.

"Hey, Bridge—oof!" Bridget had nearly jumped onto him and would have squeezed the air from his lungs if not for his protective armor.

"I had a vision, Landon!" Bridget stepped back, raising her palms. "Of this!" She flung out her arms and gestured around as if she had created the scenery. Then she pointed at Vates's leaf-boat. "And of that!"

For the first time, Landon had a good chance to really look at it: the rigid, cupped green leaf with its canopy of pink patches stitched together. Vates sat in the boat like a child eagerly awaiting a ride at the amusement park.

"You saw that?" Landon said, amazed and still bewildered.

Bridget nodded. "As soon as we found the Rose—isn't it *be-you-tea-full?*—I looked up and saw parachutes coming down, although they weren't real. I only saw them. And they were chess pieces like the one Grandpa made in the barn."

"Jalopy," Landon said, looking around for the horse.

"Yes," said Bridget. "With parachutes like we had falling from the barn. And while I was still looking up, a petal fell from the flower just like a parachute. And then a leaf fell, too." Bridget made a shocked face and leaned back. "Bang! The leaf didn't float. It fell hard."

Landon was shaking his head. "So you decided to put them together to make these." He waved at Vates's leaf-boat.

Bridget nodded, then stopped. "Well, once we found the spider. Or it found us. Yes. I told some of the ladies about what I'd seen, and they went right to work with pine needles and spider-web thread making puffy-chutes"—she indicated the canopy's patchwork—"instead of smooth parachutes. I guess they hold the air better?" She shrugged.

"It's so beautiful," said Vates, watching Landon and Bridget from the leaf-boat. "And it's brilliant." His gray hair lifted gently from the river breeze. As he looked about, he was no longer giggling but sighing. Breathing in the scenery, the moment, and something else, and then letting out the deepest, fullest, most contented sigh Landon had ever heard. Not only a sigh of contentment. Vates was full of joy. He was mumbling something as he looked back at Landon and Bridget.

"What's that?" said Landon, losing the old man's words to the din of the crowd and the soft slap of water along the boat.

"To have the faith and hope and vision of a child," Vates said, smiling. He looked directly at Bridget. "I'll need another passenger, young lady."

Bridget nodded and looked at Landon. "Once we made the first boat, the leaves kept falling, and we kept making more boats until the leaves stopped. Epops flew back as we finished the last boat, and he said to leave it up there by the Rose for Vates and you."

What had been puzzling Landon was now becoming clear. His own vision of the Auctor-as-man forming from rose petals in the air beyond the waterfall took on new meaning. "The Rose signifies the Auctor. He gave us the petals and the leaves to carry us to his kingdom." Landon gulped. "Out over the waterfall."

Landon looked at Vates. They had been through so much together. There was so much Landon wanted to thank him for, beginning with the Auctor's Riddle that had first led Landon to this magical realm. Instead, they merely gazed at one another for a long moment, covering more than words could say with their silent stare. Vates slowly nodded, and Landon did the same.

"Aye-yip! Aye-yee! Excuse me! Sorry!"

Ludo emerged from the crowd all pointy elbows and knees. When he reached the bank, he paused, elbows back like chicken wings, and he gasped at the sight of the river. " 'Tis true indeed, from what Ditty did read." Ludo gaped and then clamped his bared teeth as if biting a rope. Feister the ferret zipped from behind Ludo's back to jut from his shoulder like a bowsprit, his tiny nose twitching.

It felt like Vates stood, although he had only leaned forward, hunching in the leaf-boat. "So does our mischievous Ludo finally believe?"

Ludo's body remained a frozen frame of angles and joints, while his eyes wavered to and fro along the river and then back to Vates. The crowd fell hush. The river slapped. Ludo's teeth unclamped. "Yes. I guess."

"Ho, Ludo!" the crowd erupted. "Bravo, Vates!"

Vates smiled and slid to one side of the boat. With one open hand he gestured toward the open space beside him. Room enough for one more. Or two, if one of them was a ferret.

The crowd continued to cheer and clap as Ludo stepped tentatively into the boat. He hunkered down, unsure, until Vates patted him on the back. Then Ludo's hard edges softened, and he appeared to both melt and bloom. He bent down, ducking from view before coming up holding the ball end of the towing line. Pitching the ball toward shore, Ludo said his final word of farewell: "Heave!"

"Ho, Ludo!"

"Bravo, Vates!"

The leaf-boat twisted and floated away, heading downstream. As the crowd roared and clapped, Landon felt his mouth grow dry with speechlessness. When the leaf-boat rounded a bend, vanishing behind the trees, Landon finally laughed. Then he clapped, waving the Rose shield. "Now that was the oddest sight I've ever seen," he muttered to himself. "Vates and Ludo together as friends." Landon looked up and smiled. "The Auctor does work miracles."

Holly had come out during the commotion and stood by Bridget and Landon. "Amazing," Holly said.

Landon turned around. "Yeah. Who would have guessed *that*? Seeing them together."

"No," said Holly. "I don't mean them. I just finished counting the leaf-boats and got a head count of the people and animals here. Given the size of the boats and the number of creatures that can fit in each one, we have precisely enough boats for everyone. Not one more, and not one less."

"Did you count the birds, too?" asked Bridget.

"Birds?" Holly looked at her. "I haven't seen any, except for Epops."

"Oh, yeah," said Bridget shaking her head. "The birds already left."

"You saw them?" said Landon. "Where were they?"

Bridget raised her hands toward the sky. "Everywhere! When we first got here, there were so many birds"—she glanced at Holly—"it would have been impossible to count them all."

"Twee-too! Twee-twee-too!" Epops fluttered into view and alighted on Bridget's shoulder. The little green bird cocked his head and chirped and sang and chirped while Bridget inclined her ear, nodding. After chirping good-bye to Landon and Holly, Epops took off in a bouncing flight down the river and out of view.

"It's official," said Bridget importantly. "All of the birds are now gone. Epops was going to catch up to Vates and Ludo. And Feister." She grinned.

A touch of loneliness pressed on Landon's heart. Now that they were here, everything seemed to be happening so fast. The birds, which he hadn't even gotten another chance to see, had all flown away. Ludo and Vates and now Epops were gone. At least Bridget's company had waited for them. At least he could see everyone else as they departed. And it was time to depart. He knew that. This was it. The Arcans would be coming down the hill any moment. It was time to evacuate Wonderwood and leave this realm. . .forever.

"Bridget," Landon said. "I've been wondering why everyone here is so calm. Happy even. I mean the Arcans are still after us. We should probably hurry with the evacuation."

Bridget listened with a serious expression, almost mocking, and then she grinned again.

"What is it?" asked Landon. "Is there a joke?"

Bridget shook her head, biting her lip. "I didn't tell you how we got all those sails stitched so fast. The valley people work wonders with needle and thread. But we also made friends with some new creatures."

"New creatures? Holly, did you know about this?" Landon looked at his other sister.

"We, uh, met some of them on the way down the hill." She closed her eyes and shuddered. Bridget giggled.

"You know how big the Rose is?" Bridget asked. "Well, we met some spiders who are—" She looked to Holly for help.

"Of the same proportion," Holly said. "Meaning they're huge."

"And what do these spiders have to do with the Arcans?" Landon asked.

"The spiders are waiting in the trees for them. When you and Vates came down in your boat? That was the signal for Aran to set up her net across the whole hill. The other spiders were laying traps, too."

"Aran?" said Landon. "Who is that?"

"The Spider Queen."

Landon mimicked Holly's shudder. He was glad he hadn't seen the monster spiders waiting in the trees. He was also glad the spiders were on their side. Another thought crossed Landon's mind, and he looked to the sky.

"Are the spiders and their webs heat resistant?"

Bridget shrugged. "Why?"

"Volucer Ignis," said Landon. "I'm surprised he hasn't shown up yet."

As he studied the sky, watching for signs of the dragon, a vision appeared. It was the Rose, and as in his previous vision of it, white petals were falling. This time, rather than catching on the Rose's thorns, the falling petals were caught and torn by dragon claws. The stem became Volucer Ignis's neck. The flower became a plume of fire. The Rose was gone. Volucer Ignis remained, leering.

"What's wrong, Landon?" Holly and Bridget were looking at him.

"What? Oh." He looked down from the sky, but he was still lost in the vision. Finally, he heard the sound of the river flowing by and smelled the fresh clean air. The sky was still blue.

A faint hum came from his shield and the sword at his hip. It felt like a soft electric current. Drawing the sword from its scabbard and turning the shield, Landon wondered if the river water had begun to wash the Rose and stem emblems away. They had both faded against the smooth steel. As he watched, the stem on the sword writhed like a dragon's tail, and the flower and split leaves over the shield distorted into a grotesque face, glinting fire. Landon almost threw down the shield and weapon, afraid they might burn his arms.

"Landon? What is going on?"

"Don't you see it?" Landon said, staring at the devices.

"What?" said Holly. "They look fine. Beautiful, actually. Look at that Rose—"

Landon yanked the shield away. "Don't touch it!" He backed up, glaring madly. "It's not a rose. It's the dragon."

Holly and Bridget stared at Landon, their mouths open. Thankfully, others had taken charge of the crowd—Ravusmane and Hardy, perhaps—and were directing people and animals alike to the flotilla of waiting leaf-boats. Someone came over, a stocky man in coveralls Landon didn't recognize, asking to borrow Bridget's dagger. She pulled out the blade and handed it to him. The man nodded repeatedly and glanced shyly at Landon before saying thank you and moving away.

"What was that about?" said Landon.

"To cut the netting so the boats can sail," Bridget explained. She still wore a concerned expression over Landon's dragon comment, as did Holly.

Landon looked at the shield. The dragon's head didn't move, but the tint of fire in his eyes and mouth and nostrils appeared to waver. It was probably just a play of the light. "You really don't see it?" Landon asked. He was as astonished as his sisters.

Holly sighed. "I see the Rose. And on your sword, the Rose stem."

What could this mean? Suddenly, Landon said, "He's letting us get away."

"What?"

"Volucer Ignis," Landon said, looking up. "He likes to play games. He's letting everyone get away on the boats. They'll sail over the waterfall, you know. And then they'll just be sitting, or floating ducks. Totally helpless and defenseless in the air. That's why he's not attacking us here. It's got to be."

"You think he's going to destroy everyone in the air?" said Bridget. For the first time since Landon's arrival at the river, his little sister's face looked doubtful.

Landon nodded. "He's waiting until we're all gone. He wants us to escape. Then he can kill us. And then when we're all gone, he'll go after the Rose."

Holly shook her head. "I still don't get it. Are you sure? Maybe he's afraid of the river. This is Shay Run. It flows down from the mountain. Your sword and shield look fine to me."

Landon looked at the water. It was remarkably pure. Were it not moving, they would be able to see right through it to its depths. Looking from the water to the shield, he again saw the Rose. As soon as he wondered about it, however, the flower faded and twisted into the dragon's head.

"I think our belief and hope in the Rose is what helps it grow," said Landon. "Like water and sunshine. If we die before reaching the Auctor's Kingdom, then the Rose will wither, and

Volucer Ignis will have won."

"I hate that dragon," Bridget said stamping her foot. "He's always trying to ruin everything."

"It's a test," Landon said, twisting the sword and thinking aloud. "The prophecy said the final test would come at the Rose. And it's *my* test. I'm the one who will have to face him."

Cheers broke out as the shimmering net was cut loose and the leaf-boats, each carrying at least two passengers, began to drift apart, gliding with the current. It was like watching a dream pass by, these giant leaves with pink-petal canopies bearing people and animals downriver. Landon wanted to join in their cheers and return their happy waves, but with each passing boat he felt his heart growing heavier.

"I will not let them down. I will not let them die. I came back to this world to save them, and"—Landon's voice broke, but he quickly recovered—"I will do my duty, and be glad for it."

"Hey," Holly said, stepping forward. "*We* came back to save them. All three of us. Remember in Grandpa Karl's study? We agreed and decided—together—to come back."

Bridget looked at Landon and Holly and then turned and ran away.

"Hey!" Holly shouted after her. "Where are you going, Bridget?"

"To get my sword!" she called over her shoulder. "Wait for me!"

Chapter Seventeen

Landon watched Bridget race to the net cutter to retrieve her sword. The stocky man handed it to her, bowing. Then he and a little lady, his wife perhaps, climbed into a leaf-boat. Bridget shoved them off and waved good-bye as they drifted happily downstream. The white horses and dark brown one— Ghost, Snowflake, and Jalopy—stood farther down the shore, taking turns lapping water.

Most of the boats were gone. For a while, the river had been cluttered with them, the air filled with boisterous laughter and chattering. Despite the multitude of boats, the water was wide enough so that it never threatened to jam. A few boats had been anchored individually to shore. Landon presumed these awaited him and his sisters, their horses, and the last remaining people of Wonderwood. The world was getting to seem an empty place.

A couple bears squeezing into one boat made for a funny

picture. Holly giggled and waved as the black animals waved and growled. Bridget ran apace with the bears' boat, waving and shouting "Thank you! Thanks again! Bye!"

Three people knelt along the shore after seeing others safely off. It was Ditty with her parents. Hardy and Wagglewhip emerged at the top of the bank and clambered down toward the water. Behind them padded Ravusmane, his gray head and bushy tail held high. They approached Landon.

"Dose spideys got de Arcans all tangledy." Hardy's crooked teeth poked out as he grinned. "Dey're wrapped like big flies, wid deir swords stuck like dis." He held his arm out and froze, pretending to struggle to move it. "Ungh, ungh," Hardy grunted, making a funny face and roving his eyes.

Holly and Bridget giggled, and Bridget stroked Ravusmane's fur.

"Did you see the dragon?" Landon asked.

Hardy held his ridiculous pose another moment and shook his head, lowering his arm.

"I didn't either," said Wagglewhip. He was rubbing his forearm where he had a crude tattoo of a skull and crossbones, which he was deeply ashamed of. "Only the spiders taking care of those Arcans."

Something drew Landon's attention from the corner of his eye. Ditty, kneeling by her parents, was watching him. When he looked at her, she bowed her head, continuing to pray.

Ravusmane said, "Volucer Ignis prowls the sky. He's circling the Rose. There's nothing else left on the hilltop. Only the Rose surrounded by ashes. Why he keeps to the sky out of sight I do not understand."

Everyone looked at Landon as if he might have an answer. He kept glancing toward Ditty, whose head was still down. Landon held out his sword and shield. "What do you see?" he asked the three scouts.

The three of them stared, their eyes narrowing. Hardy sniffed as if he were about to cry. "Dose are beautiful," he said.

Landon sneaked a peek at the shield and saw the dragon. He quickly flipped it back.

"Well!" Wagglewhip suddenly rubbed his hands on his coveralls. "I suppose it's time to bid farewell." He began to turn when Landon reached out and grabbed his arm. Wagglewhip winced, not in pain but because Landon's thumb was pressing just below his ugly tattoo.

"Thank you, Wagglewhip," said Landon. He looked at the tattoo and then up at Wagglewhip's apprehensive face and smiled. "Really."

"Really?" Wagglewhip raised his eyebrows.

Landon nodded. "Really." He waited for Wagglewhip to relax before he let go of his arm.

Bridget and Holly each gave Wagglewhip a hug, provoking slobbery sniffs from him before he jogged away to the boats. Ravusmane was next.

"You found us on the mountain and brought us safely to the wall. We couldn't have done it without your help."

The gray wolf retreated a step and bowed his head. "The satisfaction is mine, Landon Snow." He looked up at the three children. "Take care of each other, and always be on the lookout." Raising his muzzle he sniffed the air. "Vigilance is a virtue." He was nearly toppled over by Bridget's hug. She had set her sword and armor aside.

"I wish we could take you with us, Ravusmane. I like talking with you."

"Keep the faith, little miss. And keep listening. You never know what you might hear."

"I will," Bridget said, sniffling. "I'll miss you."

After Holly and Landon petted him, they said their final good-byes, and Ravusmane trotted off, leaving Hardy alone with the Snow children. The four of them stood quietly together, listening to the water passing by. Finally, Hardy spoke.

"I knew dere was someding special about you first time I spied you under Ludo's tree. Remember dat? You and—"

Hardy broke off, looking down. "You and your horsy."

Landon sighed. "I'll never forget. You were late to Ludo's circle. 'Tardy Hardy' they called you. And when you fell out of the tree, I thought you were a pinecone."

Hardy glanced up uncertainly. "Really? A pinecone?"

Landon nodded. "Whump!" he said, stamping. "You hit the ground and then came in with that funny hat on. I thought, well. . ."

Hardy wrinkled his forehead, waiting.

"Well," Landon continued. "I didn't think you were as smart as you are, at first. But you're one of the smartest of all."

"Oh, now, I wouldn't know about all *dat*," Hardy said with mock humility. After swishing his foot around in the dirt, he glanced up sharply and shot Landon his signature wink. And Landon smiled.

Landon and Hardy shook hands and then embraced, patting

one another's back like old war buddies, which is what they were.

"I'm sorry about Melech," said Hardy. "He was quite a horsy for you and me. But mostly you. I always wondered how you get him here."

It'd been so long and Landon had gotten so used to Melech being in Wonderwood that he often forgot Melech wasn't a creature from this realm. Landon pointed at the other horses. "Like them," he said. "From a chessboard in the sky. Or our grandfather's barn," he added.

Hardy frowned.

Holly and Bridget hugged him together, and then, sniffing back tears, Hardy trudged down the shore. After a brief discussion, Hardy and Wagglewhip climbed into the same boat, Hardy wading out with it before pulling himself up and in. Seeing the two former Odds sailing down the river, Landon knew things would never be the same again.

Five leaf-boats remained moored by separate lines of thick thread to sticks in the mud. Landon walked alone toward Ditty and her parents. Ditty rose quickly and met him halfway. The river water reflected in her round eyes, even pooling in their rims. She was trying to smile, but her lips kept quivering downward instead of up.

"I wish you could come back to our world, Ditty." Landon stopped, eyeing the leaf-boats. "What if you *can?* If we rode in the same boat together—"

Ditty was shaking her head, her soft hair swishing back and forth. She was hugging her book, the *Book of Illumination*, to her chest.

"It's not possible," she said. Without further explanation, Landon knew in his heart that she was right. "There's something else I need to tell you, Landon. I should have told you before, but I didn't want to. I was afraid. I'm sorry." She closed her eyes, pursing her lips.

Landon moved to set down his shield, glancing at it to see the leering dragon, and then took hold of Ditty's thin shoulders.

"What is it? What do you want to tell me?"

"I should have told you everything that I'd read. Vates was leaving it to me to tell you because I asked him to. And then he seemed so happy, like a burden had been lifted from him. But the burden's still there. And I have it, and so do you."

"What?" said Landon. "What is it? I don't care that you haven't told me. I mean, I'm not mad, Ditty."

She opened her eyes, which were puffy and glistening. "The final test comes down to the Rose and the dragon."

Landon studied her. "Right. You did say that, I think."

She tightened her lips. "It's a battle of faith"—she took a deep breath—"between two from the outside. It's destiny that you meet there. And there our destiny"—she spread her hands—"will be decided."

Landon held her shoulders firmly. "Wait a second. *Two* from the outside? What do you mean?"

" 'One with the shadows, one with the light. The one serving the dragon will come to the Rose for the final fight.' "

Landon stared at her, breathless. This couldn't be right, could it? Did Ditty actually mean that he was supposed to face—

Landon whispered his name. "Max?"

Ditty's tense chin pushed out her lower lip. She nodded. "It must be him."

Landon let go of her shoulders, slumping his own. "But I don't get it. How is it a test of faith?"

"Your faith in the Auctor against his faith in Volucer Ignis."

Landon rubbed his chin and scratched his head beneath his helmet. He felt dizzy and warm. "Max," he said blankly. "I thought it was all about the dragon, not a boy from Button Up—"

"It is about the dragon and the Rose *here*," Ditty said. "But it's up to you—or Max—to decide which one lives. The fate of Wonderwood still lies in your hands. Or rather"—Ditty reached out and pressed her hand on Landon's chest—"in your heart."

Landon gasped at her touch, then shuddered. "I've been seeing the dragon, Volucer Ignis, in my shield."

Ditty withdrew her hand a moment, then put it back. "Max's confidence in the evil one has been building. But we've been praying for you, Landon."

"How can I beat him? What should I do? Am I *supposed* to kill Max?"

Ditty kept her hand on his chest. "I don't know. All I do know is that your faith has brought you this far, and us with you. And the Auctor is worthy of more faith yet." At last, her chin relaxed and her lip stopped quivering. She smiled.

Landon nodded. "I've got a job to do. My final task here." He looked around, noticing how the scenery seemed to change with every glance. Was it fading? Or merely waiting? "My final test."

Ditty stared at him solemnly. Finally she removed her hand. They embraced, but not for very long. A space was already coming between them, a distance that they both knew would only grow. Yet no matter how far apart time and space would take them, they also knew they would always be together in their shared faith and adventures.

"I won't forget you, Ditty," Landon said. A mixture of pain and excitement stirred him, propelling him back a step. And then another.

Ditty smiled. "I have faith in you, too. And you have my prayers."

In the background, her parents rose from the riverbank. They never came into clear focus again, although Landon did see them raise their arms to wave. He kept his eyes on Ditty as he backed up, raising his sword in a final salute. Ditty's parents moved toward the water and climbed into a leaf-boat together. Ditty backed away, too, her eyes and features blurring. She climbed into a boat and was joined by Ravusmane, and they sailed down the river after her parents. Her face followed Landon as he ascended the bank and stepped into the wood. He could feel her gaze going with him even as the river disappeared from view.

"Hey!" a girl's voice shouted.

"We're coming, too!" yelled another.

As Holly and Bridget stepped along either side of him, huffing, Landon kept his eyes on the path ahead. "We've got a job to do," he said. "And I don't even know what it is."

"Three boats," said Holly distractedly.

"What?" said Landon, trying to keep his focus.

"There are only three leaf-boats left in the river. It looks pretty lonely down there."

Landon sighed. "Not as lonely as it's going to look up here, I'm afraid," he muttered.

The only activity in the wood was high in the trees, where giant spiders continued bundling Arcans. The web-wrapped mummies were everywhere, blotting the treetops. Arcan swords and helmets littered the ground. Occasionally, a muffled scream sounded. One Arcan mummy, dangling by a thread and being drawn up in starts, was squirming. What at first Landon thought to be leaves rustling turned out to be busy spider legs bustling. The noise was getting to Landon so that he could feel it along his spine and up his neck. He shuddered, concentrating on the path ahead. Grateful as he was for the spiders, he was also glad he didn't have to see one up close.

Chapter Eighteen

Through the eerily quiet wood, they reached the charred hilltop, which was completely scorched as Ravusmane had reported. The sky overhead was a black swirl. Landon, Holly, and Bridget were stepping into a world as bleak and dark as the riverbank had been bright and active. Even the giant Rose looked forlorn amid the ashes. It certainly looked out of place for its size and color in this barren, dead site.

"All the trees are gone," Bridget whispered. The wind picked up, spraying dust into their faces. Bridget sneezed.

As Landon gazed at the black sky, he felt the weight of his shield and the sword resting against his hip. Was the shield really a shield of faith? Would it protect him? Or did it merely *reflect* his faith? Landon was tempted to look at it, wondering if he would find the bloom of a rose or the face of a dragon. Closing his eyes, Landon went deep inside himself. He had memorized verses from his Bible. He was searching for these verses on the pages of his heart. To face the dragon and Max, Landon needed words from the Auctor to go along with his sword.

Finally a page settled, and Landon saw underlined words rising from the page: "Be strong and of good courage, fear not, nor be afraid of them: for the LORD thy God, he it is that doth go with thee; he will not fail thee, nor forsake thee" (Deuteronomy 31:6).

Opening his eyes, Landon felt his whole body relax, and the shield slipped from his loosened grasp. It fell facedown in the ashes with a gentle *poof.* A small cloud of dust rose up.

Bridget and Holly both bent to retrieve it, but Landon told them no. "I'm seeing another verse," he said, stretching his hand. "Hold on." He closed his eyes, and the page was there before him: "For we walk by faith, not by sight" (2 Corinthians 5:7).

"I don't need the shield," Landon said. "And I don't want to see it." He opened his eyes and looked at his bewildered sisters. "It's okay," he said grinning. "If it comes to a point where we need the shield, then it's probably too late anyway."

Holly and Bridget looked at each other, unsure.

"So what are we going to do?" said Holly. "We came here to stop Volucer Ignis once and for all, right? So how can we kill him?"

The sky rumbled, and a fuzzy streak of orange lightning followed. The showdown was about to occur.

"Hold my hands," said Landon suddenly. When the girls hesitated, he grasped their closest hands, and then Holly and Bridget joined their other hands, closing the loop.

"We're not going to sing, are we?" Holly asked dryly. "This hardly seems the time or the place."

Landon squinted at her. "We'll sing afterward. How about that? You can do the first solo, Holly."

Holly rolled her eyes.

"Are we going to pray?" Bridget asked.

"Yes." Landon nodded. "Silently. See what the Auctor tells you. Or shows you." He gave each of his sisters an earnest look and lifted his head and closed his eyes.

Landon saw two names, neither of which he recognized. One of the characters drew a bow and killed the other, the arrow going right through his heart.

But then Landon saw these words following: "Thou shalt love thy neighbour as thyself."

Landon felt a squeeze on his left hand and then another squeeze on his right. Silently, Holly and Bridget retreated into the wood. A minute later, they returned, followed by a lumbering, clicking spider.

Landon couldn't help staring at the spider's many eyes and its arcing, jointed legs. It looked like it was climbing rather than walking. Fingerlike teeth worked in its mouth. Landon tried not to gag. It was their friend, after all.

Still, Landon's body grew tense as the spider approached. Thankfully, it stopped several yards away, where Bridget spoke to it, pointing at the Rose and then to either side of it. The spider seemed to nod, its entire body bobbing between its legs. Then it froze, hunched down, and sprang into the air. It landed high on the Rose stem and clambered up onto a leaf.

Two leaves below the magnificent bloom formed a near-perfect ninety-degree angle, cupping the reddish pink flower like two hands, much like the leaves had appeared on the shield. These leaves were larger than the ones used for leaf-boats. If each leaf-boat could carry two bears, the two leaves near the flower could hold twenty apiece.

The spider was out at the leftmost tip, defying gravity as it worked over and under and around the leaf. Soon it crawled across the stem to the leaf on the right-hand side, where it busied itself at the tip of that leaf. Given the height and size of the Rose, the spider didn't appear large at all.

When the spider finished its work on the right, it moved back toward the center of the stem. Except it wasn't crawling on the flower; it was walking in midair. Or so it appeared.

Landon could see Holly and Bridget standing next to him out of the corner of his eye. They, too, were staring up at the spider's tightrope act.

"What is it doing?" Landon asked. "Making a web to catch the dragon?"

"We're not sure," Holly said. "But Bridget and I both saw the same thing when we prayed. Didn't we, Bridge?"

"Yeah," said Bridget. "A web between two leaves. Just like that."

"How come he stopped?" Landon wasn't sure whether to call the spider he or she. "Is the web finished?" It didn't look like much from down here.

"Not quite," said Holly. "Look. She's dropping a line."

She. Landon made a mental note in case he might need to address the spider personally.

Holly and Bridget jogged forward until they were under the

descending thread. Were they going up there? Should Landon go, too? But they didn't climb on. Rather, they wrapped the thread around their swords, Bridget's short dagger first, and then Holly's midsize blade. After giving it several twists to make sure it was secure, Holly tugged on the thread while Bridget cupped her hands around her mouth and shouted, "Okay! Up, up and away!"

As their swords began to rise, Landon wondered if Ditty and Ravusmane had reached the waterfall. Volucer Ignis was waiting, circling above the Rose until the last citizens of Wonderwood had vacated this world. The prophecy dictated that. The final battle was to be waged between two boys from another world. Whoever had more faith in his master would win.

Landon sighed heavily, then took another deep breath. He glanced at the shield lying facedown in the ashes. Should he look at it to see what it would reveal? No, he decided. He had to trust the Auctor alone, without looking for a sign on a shield.

He drew in another deep breath.

The twist of swords was barely visible as it reached the spider, just a tiny dot going up. The spider retrieved it and seemed to be doing something with the swords. What would a spider want with the girls' swords? Holly and Bridget stepped back, gazing up. The sky beyond the Rose looked like oily coffee being stirred. A warm breeze descended.

"It's getting close," Landon said. "Volucer Ignis is preparing to make a move soon. I can feel it." He tightened his grip on the hilt of his sword.

The spider remained in its position between the spread

leaves. It appeared to be done with whatever it was doing with the swords. Now what?

Something glistened or wavered beneath the spider. She was lowering another thread. As Landon squinted to follow the lowering line, he heard a horse whinnying in the distance.

"Melech!" Landon gasped. "Look out!"

He didn't actually say the words. He heard them in his own voice as if a recording were being played back in his head.

Melech!

Look out!

Landon could see Melech running into the tunnel of flames. Then he knew what he would do.

Landon ran to the dropping thread, telling Holly and Bridget to join him.

"We need to pull this down, all the way down," he said.

"We just sent our swords *up*," Holly protested.

"And do you know *why?*" Landon looked at her, and she shrugged. "So that I can send my sword up, too." He smiled at his sister's frown. "Come on. It'll get hard the closer we get it to us, but we can't let go. All right?"

Holly and Bridget nodded.

The three of them worked hand over hand, drawing the sticky rope downward. It felt like they were winning at tug of war. But as Landon had warned, the battle grew harder. Soon Bridget was grunting, and then Holly was groaning, and Landon started murmuring through gritted teeth, "Come on, come on, *come on!*" His fingers ached, his hands felt stiff, and his arms and shoulders began to tighten. But he could not let go. He would not let go.

The spider remained where she was, which meant she was gradually descending toward them while her web between the leaves stretched taut. She had woven Bridget's dagger and Holly's sword into the web beneath her so that the blades and handles formed something of a narrow rectangle. As much as Landon didn't want to have the spider on top of him or see her underside this close up, her weight helped their effort to draw the web to the ground.

"She needs to stay on—*ungh*—until the last instant. Can one of you tell her that?" Landon felt sweat trickle down his back. He heard a strange clicking and smacking and then realized Bridget was talking to the spider. He didn't even want to see Bridget's mouth.

"She'll stay as long as you want, Landon," said Bridget. "Tack tock."

"Good," said Landon. "What was that?"

"She said thank you," Holly explained, "to the spider."

"Oh." Landon thought of trying to mimic Bridget but then thought better of it in case he didn't make the noises right. Instead of thanking the spider, he might accidentally say something offensive. And he did not want to offend this spider.

"Tell her thanks from me, too," he said.

"Tacks *took*."

The spider wriggled her legs, clicking like an out-of-whack turn signal. Landon thought he was going to be sick. Then the spider was on the ground, her web stretching to the leaves jutting on either side of the Rose. Landon and his sisters were panting. The spider's multiple eyes studying them all at once.

"Tacks *took*," Landon said without thinking. "Tacks took to you and you," he said to Holly and Bridget, "too."

The girls barely nodded. They were applying all their strength to keeping the spider down on her web.

Landon knelt on the web beneath the spider's mouth, pressing a knee to either side of the narrow rectangle of swords. He carefully slid his own sword out. He laid it flat on the web so he wouldn't cut any threads by mistake. Gradually, he raised the blade, placing the hilt in the notch of the rectangle until it was pointing straight up at the spider's head. Landon held his sword in position, hooking his fingers over the edges of the hilt, balancing the steel blade.

The spider's mouth made one dull click and stopped moving. Her eyes all seemed fixed on the sword pointed at her.

"It's okay," Landon said as soothingly as he could with all his muscles as taut and tense as the extended web. "Just—a—lit–tle— lon–ger." Sweat dripped from his face.

The air grew warmer, thicker. Stifling.

A gust kicked up the ashes.

Bridget gasped and collapsed, her body spent.

A moment later, Holly shrieked, "Cramp!" and rolled away, clutching her calf. She kept rolling and writhing in pain.

Landon thought he'd go blind from the intensity. There was no way he could hold the web down by himself, even with the spider's weight. Without his sisters, he had to move his knees back and press the web with his elbows while still balancing the sword with his fingers. It was a miracle something didn't snap. Either him or the web.

It's not my own strength, he kept thinking. *There's no way I can do this!*

How much longer could he hold on?

Faith.

I trust you, Auctor. And I trust that only you can do this. Only you can destroy Volucer Ignis. I don't have the strength to fight anymore.

Yet Landon kept holding on.

How long was he kneeling there, elbows dug into the ash through the web, hands holding onto a sword he couldn't afford to let tip, head lifting and then drooping from fatigue? How long?

How long?

Chapter Nineteen

When Landon looked up, the spider was gone. Bridget had passed out. Holly lay in a contorted ball, grimacing and kneading her leg.

How long had he been in this position? When had the spider left him? The Rose appeared to be turning. But it was actually the sky, black and spinning. Landon felt dizzy, sick to his stomach.

Still he held on.

You came, didn't you, he said in his mind to the Auctor. *You yourself were here. You. . .you went through even more than this, didn't you? How did you do it? How could you stand it?*

Ash was getting in Landon's eyes. He couldn't rub them. It sifted into his nose and mouth and ears. He was getting thirsty. Oh how refreshing the water in the river had been! How sweet it would taste right now. He might get there yet, if he could hold on a little longer. A flat or flipping sword would do no good at all. He had seen Melech rush straight into the dragon's gaping mouth, straight and true. Landon knew that was the only way to defeat Volucer Ignis. A direct, piercing shot through his own fire and into his heart. The rest of his grotesque body was too well protected. Even a strike to one of his eyes would only wound him. Annoy him. Anger him. It wouldn't kill him.

The Auctor's sword must find the heart of the dragon.

Landon could only wait. And hope.

A dust cloud rose in front of him and puffed away. Landon thought he saw his book, his Bible fluttering there. Its pages riffling and turning. He couldn't come up with memorized verses on his own. His mind was exhausted along with his body. There was really nothing left. And so he looked at his Bible and waited for a page to come. Underlined words. A final message for him from the Auctor.

And there it was. There were words. Landon licked his dried lips and blinked, trying to wet his coated eyes. Through the blowing dust he made out one word at a time.

Love
Thy
Neighbour
As
Thyself

The Bible faded. The words were gone. But not from Landon's memory. It was all he could see, all he could think about. In Button Up, his grandparents' neighbors were the Westmorelands. So they were Landon's neighbors, too. That's what the verse meant. The Auctor was telling him that he was supposed to love Max, the boy riding the dragon. The problem was Landon didn't even *like* Max. What was to like—or love—in him? He was mean. He had tried to kill Landon and his sisters and Humphrey, their great-great-great-great-grandfather, when they had traveled back in time. Max's family had been after the Button Up Library and other property since the day it was built. They were greedy. Selfish. Nasty—

Love them. . .

Was this part of the test? What more could Landon do? What did loving a nasty kid have to do with faith?

Landon felt like he was having an out-of-body experience. He was looking at himself kneeling on the stretched web—the world's tallest slingshot. His fingertips balanced the sword precariously. His head was bowed. The Rose reached up and up into the black whirl of sky. It seemed he could feel nothing. Only watch and wait.

Was he already dead?

And what about Holly and Bridget? They looked dead, or near to it, too. Perhaps the Rose petals would fall and cover them, and this would be their burial ground.

How could Landon kill Volucer Ignis while loving Max? Max was riding the dragon. He was one with the beast for all evil purposes. What was Landon to do even if he had a shot?

"Trust in me."

Yeah, Landon thought. *Trust you.*

"Have faith."

I do! Look at me!

"Love your neighbor."

I can't, Landon thought. *I can't love him. I can love my sisters and my parents. I love my grandparents. I can love Vates and Hardy and Ditty. I loved Melech. But how can I love my enemy?*

"*Your enemy is not flesh and blood. Leave your enemy to me.* Max *is flesh and blood. I created him, as well as you.*"

This just didn't seem possible. It didn't make sense. Landon never thought this test would prove so hard. So impossible.

Do you love him? Landon asked the Auctor.

"*Yes.*"

You haven't given up on Max?

"*No.*"

Did the sky stop swirling? Or was it only Landon's imagination? Was all of this real? Or was he having a strange dream? No, the black sky was twirling. . .but something was different.

Inside Landon's heart, something tripped like a switch. He saw Max in a new way, a new light he had not seen before. *The Auctor loves him.* Landon couldn't do it, but the Auctor could.

To love him, Landon pondered, *do I need to forgive him?*

"*Yes. Forgiveness unstops the flow of love. Bitterness chokes it.*"

The sky was clearing from the outside in. The darkness whirled in the other direction like black oil running down a drain. It was collecting in one spot where a dot grew darker and darker. Finally that was all that was left: a black dot in an otherwise clear sky above the Rose of Shay Run. Then the black dot grew. It wasn't spreading again; it was descending.

I trust you, Landon told the Auctor.

The black dot took the form of a dragon, his wings spread and his tail straight up.

I have faith in you, Landon said in his heart.

LANDON SNOW AND THE AUCTOR'S KINGDOM

The dragon was dive-bombing the Rose. His face came into view, darker than ever before. It was Volucer Ignis, but he looked different. No trace of reason or personality was left in his face. He was a monster ruled by hatred. The master of demons, hoarding them within his wingspan. A black blur followed his descent, a shadowy contrail. His eyes shimmered, glowing with fire. Or were they reflecting a dual image of the Rose?

Max clung to the dragon's back, terrified. He was trying to grasp something beyond his control. Being taken down on a spiraling ride to death.

How could Landon see all this? He couldn't, yet he could. He could see himself and his sisters. He could see the marvelous Rose. He could see the black plunging dragon with his helpless passenger. And he could see the Auctor glancing up from the book. He was the Author and Creator of life. And he was the planter of the Rose. The Rose stem glimmered green. Then Landon realized he was kneeling in the ashes, looking at his sword.

And I forgive Max.

The dragon opened his jaws, pouring out fire ahead of him. The fire engulfed the flower, racing down the stem in a blistering wave of heat. The wait was over. It would soon be finished. What faith came down to in the end, Landon learned, was not about holding on to a web or a sword or a flower or a world. But letting go.

Landon raised his elbows, leaned back, and with a slight lift of his fingers, he let go. Of everything.

For a split second, the web remained stretched in a gigantic V, from leaf to ground to leaf, with Landon's sword at the bottom point. It was just long enough for Landon to see that it hadn't been him or the girls or the spider that held it there. It was their faith. It was the fingertip of the Auctor.

When Landon released the web, his sword shot skyward like a rocket. Landon lost it in the fire, shielding his eyes. Yet he could see it flying through the raging blaze up into the dragon's mouth. The sword shot through Volucer Ignis's throat, ripping from it a silent scream. Then the sword reached the black heart. And the dragon exploded.

It was like an inverse firework. The smoke came first, shooting in all directions, followed by crackling streams of fire. And then came the boom.

The shockwave knocked the ashes from the hilltop, revealing green—if dusty—grass. When the fiery smoke cleared, the sky shined light blue. The Rose never looked so big and so beautiful.

Something else was in the sky, way up there. Landon squinted at it. A single Rose petal drifted down, although it didn't seem to be falling *normally*. It twirled and tugged and then sailed from the hilltop over the tall trees toward the river. Before it vanished from sight, Landon saw the figure hanging beneath it by means of invisible thread. Then he heard the boy's screams.

A while later as Landon let his head rest in the grass, his eyelids drooping, he thought he heard a faint splash.

Darkness.

Something was poking him. In the shoulder. The arm. It touched his cheek.

Remembering a giant spider prodding with its huge, arcing

leg, Landon rolled over and started flailing his arms. "Get off me!"

"Landon! Hey! Watch it! It's me! It's us!"

Landon opened his eyes. The first thing he saw was a rose. He thought he could reach up and touch it. It was so big, just in front of his nose. And it smelled. . .*sniff*. . .delicious. Landon raised his arm and waved through the air. Nothing. The rose was not close. It was hundreds of feet in the air! Landon sighed, smiling. Breathing in its fragrance.

It's not a rose; it's the Rose.

"You've been sleeping for about half an hour." Holly sat beside him on the grass. "Right after the explosion. We haven't been able to wake you."

"Did you see it?" Landon rolled his eyes toward his sister. He didn't feel like moving. Lying here felt so good. It was peaceful. Everything seemed peaceful.

"Incredible," said Holly.

"He blew up," said Bridget. "You blew him up, Landon. Shot him out of the sky."

Landon remembered something else. "Did you see Max?" He lifted his head.

"He took one of the boats."

Landon sat up. "What?"

Holly nodded, although her expression wasn't grim.

"He must have landed in the river. A rose petal washed up on shore, and one of the leaf-boats is gone. Our horses are still there, but only two boats are left."

"Can we make another one?" Landon asked. "What about the spiders? Can they help us make one?"

"They all left," said Holly.

"The spiders?"

Bridget nodded. "They took off. Going that way." She pointed in the direction the river was running, a parallel course through the forest.

"Two boats," said Landon, puzzling.

"We won't all fit. At least not with our horses."

"Hmm."

"And you know what else?" Holly asked. "The land is disappearing."

"What?"

"We looked over that way." Holly indicated the side of the hill where they had first come up from the plains. "Volucer Ignis had burned down a lot of the trees. But there were still some left down the hill. Now they're gone. And beyond them, uh, nothing."

"What do you mean, nothing?"

Holly shrugged. So did Bridget.

"Like nothing. Just sky. The world is shrinking."

"But the river's still there?"

"The river's still there, and the mountain across it. The mountain just goes up and up, Landon. Like land climbing into the sky."

With this world disappearing, Landon thought he should probably feel a greater sense of urgency to get going. To escape. But what was there to escape from? The evil was gone. There was no more darkness. The dragon was dead.

And so Landon felt no sense of hurry whatsoever. It was rather pleasant here, resting at the foot of the Rose.

"It smells good, doesn't it?" Landon looked at his sisters.

"I like it," said Bridget. "Reminds me of Grandma's garden."

"She does grow roses, doesn't she?" Landon muttered, remembering. Even though this world was literally fading, it seemed more real to him than ever. "I wonder if we could climb the mountain," said Landon. "What do you think we would find at the top?"

"I don't think we *could* find the top," Holly said decisively. "At least not in this lifetime. I think it goes higher than we can see."

"Wow," said Landon. "Coming from you, that's quite a statement, Holly. You think it's beyond measure? Beyond a number?"

"Infinite," said Holly. "Infinity to the third power." She grinned, and Landon smiled, not willing to cramp his brain over it.

"Three-power is funny?" Bridget knitted her brow. "Well *I* think it would smell like this. Like the flower. And like quiet."

It struck Landon that he ought to feel lonely without his friends. They were all gone. He didn't expect to see them again, at least not in this lifetime. Might he find them at the top of the mountain some day? Better than that, he would see the Auctor. And he knew that's why he felt so not alone right now. His sisters were here, yes. And so was the Auctor.

"So what do we do about the horses?" said Holly. "Flip a coin to see which one gets to go with us?"

Landon expected Bridget to be upset about leaving two horses behind. She appeared calm and relaxed, however.

"Yeah, a giant gold coin," said Landon. "If only we had one, huh? Come on. Let's go down to the river. Maybe a solution will present itself."

The shield was still lying facedown on the hill. Landon looked at it a moment and left it. His sisters, he noticed, had removed their helmets and armor and were dressed as they had been the previous morning at Grandma and Grandpa's. Not needing them anymore, Landon, too, took off his helmet, breastplate, scabbard, and leg coverings. He left them in the woods on the way down. His body felt free as a feather without the extra weight.

"What happened to the Arcans?" Landon said as they ambled down the path. High in the trees hung empty pockets of web, swaying like Spanish moss.

"Dunno," said Holly. "Looks like they were either eaten or they vanished."

"They vanished," said Bridget knowingly. When her brother and sister looked at her, she explained, "Spiders don't like Arcan. They taste bad."

The Arcan swords and helmets had vanished, too. The forest was clean, quiet, and empty. *Except not empty,* Landon thought, feeling a gentle breeze. *Full of. . .love.*

When the river came into view, Landon ran to it. Sinking to his knees, laughing, he splashed his face and arms, scooping water to his mouth and gulping. When he'd had his fill, he inhaled and closed his eyes. "Ahhh," he sighed. "Now that's good water."

Snowflake, Ghost, and Jalopy sauntered over. The Snow children patted their respective horse's nose. Snowflake whinnied, bobbing his head. And Ghost did the same.

"I think they're trying to tell us something," said Holly.

Bridget looked at her, stroking Snowflake's neck. "Of course they are," she said. "They understand the boat situation and would like to be dropped off over there." She pointed across the river.

Landon raised his eyebrows. "They *want* to be left here?"

Snowflake neighed.

Bridget gazed at her horse. "They want to climb the mountain."

It was rather like a word puzzle where one needs to get two horses across the river using only one boat. There was no real trick to it, of course, other than actually doing it without losing a boat to the current. Using the line with the knotted end that had been tossed into Vates and Landon's boat to pull them to shore, Landon managed to paddle partway across with some stiff lily pads they'd found in shallow water. Then he spotted a bush on the opposite bank and heaved the line toward it, catching on his second try and pulling him and Ghost across the rest of the way. On the return trip Holly and Bridget caught the rope and drew him in so he could rest his arms.

Bridget hugged Snowflake's neck and let him go. Once Landon had transported both white horses across the river, they mounted the bank and took off toward the vast mountain in a twin gallop.

Even though Landon and Jalopy were the biggest of the four, it seemed fitting that they go together, and Holly and Bridget ride together in the other boat. So the sisters climbed aboard, Bridget tripping and tumbling headlong into their leaf, and

Landon helped Jalopy step into his boat as Snowflake and Ghost had done. When they had cut loose from shore, the ride down the Shay Run River began.

Chapter Twenty

Holly and Bridget's leaf-boat swept out to midriver first. Landon and Jalopy followed, twisting in the current as Landon had seen normal-sized leaves do along the road after a downpour. Once their keel caught the flow, they remained more or less aligned with it, being carried with the water now faster, then slower, pausing briefly before a shallow bed of rocks before being whisked around it and speeding along again. Landon had gone canoeing and pontooning and water skiing on Minnesota lakes, and he'd floated in an inner tube down the Rum River. But he'd never sailed in a leaf before, and he had not seen a river or riverbanks so beautiful as these.

Holly and Bridget reached the river bend, and Landon heard their whoops and giggles as they sailed from view. This was better than any ride at an amusement park. By far. It was hard to describe the thrill of it and the splendor of the scenery. It was like Landon's senses had been heightened once he was on the

river. He noticed the tiniest sound of water rippling and bubbling, the faintest twinkle of sunlight from the water's surface,
each green facet of each leaf on every tree, the mixture of cool
air cruising over the water and warmer air a few feet above it, the
luxurious wetness of the water when Landon dragged his fingertips in it, and the smell—woodsy and watery and fresh—like a
potpourri dominated by the sweet perfume of the Rose. Landon
would have guessed the Rose scent would have faded by now.
Instead, it kept growing stronger and sweeter.

More than once, Landon forgot it was Jalopy riding alongside him, mistaking her for Melech. Each time, he caught himself before saying Melech's name. And each time, feeling a twinge
of sadness, he decided to say nothing. The sadness ebbed in an
instant, as fleeting as each passing tree.

When they rounded the bend, the river opened wider, an
empty superhighway of racing water. The other leaf-boat was far
ahead, shrinking in the distance. And something else was going
on. Was the river spreading indefinitely? Where were all the
trees? They hadn't all disappear—

But they had. Looking back, the trees and riverbanks behind
him had vanished, as well. There was only the river bordered by
nothing but blue sky. And way, way back rose the wall of the
mountain, from which the river flowed like a floating ribbon.
Landon thought he glimpsed two white specks on the mountain,
making their way up.

After traveling on a suspended stream of water through the
sky for a while, leaving the water altogether to continue sailing
through the air seemed only natural. As they neared the drop-off,

where a cloud of mist greeted them, Landon remembered who was with him and let out his cry of joy.

"Whoo-hoo-hoo! Jalopy! Here we go-o-o-o-o-o-*o-o-o*!"

Anyone who has gone parasailing or hang gliding knows the sensation of leaving the ground or the water to plunge upon nothing but air. And the amazing feeling when the air catches the sail to buoy the glider along. In a word, it's called flying.

After glancing back to see the waterfall dropping over nothing to an ocean about a mile below, Landon saw many other things on his journey through the air, passing over lands as grand as Wonderwood had been before the evil shadows and the Arcans and the dragon destroyed it. Other lands even more colorful and rich. People and animals—small as ants—busy about their lives. Then they passed over more ocean. Salty sea air. A small mountain range. Brisk and snowy. Rainforests. Deserts. And finally back over the sea. That is until the sea itself met a cloudy mist.

Landon held his breath as they entered the fine spray. Could it be? Was it possible the sea itself was a river? Falling toward yet another ocean filled with more exotic lands far belo—

"Ohhh!"

The leaf-boat tipped and plunged. Landon gripped the boat's side, wondering how much more his heart could take. They floated inside the mist, rising and gently falling with a wind that carried them like a child playing with a toy bird. When the fog cleared, Landon saw the most amazing sight of all.

Below them lay a cornfield, at the far end of which stood a small hill sprouting a weeping willow tree. They were descending rapidly. Landon gazed past the willow to the house and barn in the distance. His grandparents' property. He was returning to Button Up, Minnesota.

The leaf-boat skimmed the cornstalks before bumpily plunging into them. Heads of corn thudded and bounced from the boat. *Dump-dump-dump-dump-dump.* When the rose-petal chute finally snagged on the stalks, Landon jolted forward against the rim of the boat. They had come to an abrupt stop.

They?

Landon looked. Jalopy was still in the boat. She looked a little startled. But she was there.

Landon climbed out of the leaf and stood shakily amid the rows of corn. He remembered marching through the rows of Arcans when they were frozen in formation. He could think about them without fear. They were gone.

They were gone.

"Here we go. Steady, girl. That's it." Landon tried to help Jalopy out, although there was little he could offer besides verbal encouragement. She didn't have a hand to hold, and grasping her leg or hoof only made things more difficult. She made it out of the boat and looked around, making a horsy grunt.

Landon patted her nose and stroked her neck. *It's nice having a horse here,* he thought. *Had Grandma and Grandpa—or any of their ancestors—kept horses?* he wondered.

They moved through the stalks, Landon leading the way, until they reached the fence. Landon leaned on the rail, gazing at the willow on the hill. *This is where Max was when I first saw him. When we* met, *as it were.*

Landon sighed. He had forgiven Max. But old feelings were cropping up again. *Forgiveness unstops the flow; bitterness chokes it.* Landon swallowed the bitter taste and climbed over the fence. He looked at Jalopy.

"Oh. Um. Hmm." Landon scratched his head. The fence stretched a long way to either side. He decided Jalopy would have to jump it. "Do you think you can?" Landon asked after explaining what she needed to do. Then he felt silly for talking to a horse. This was Button Up, Minnesota. Not Wonderwood. Landon laughed.

But Jalopy was backing her way into the corn. When she had all but disappeared, she pawed the dirt, snorted, and charged.

Landon leaped out of the way.

Jalopy sailed over, clearing the top rail by a good foot before thundering on the other side. Landon stared, his mouth hanging open. Finally, he muttered in a raspy voice, "Good girl. Well done, Jalopy."

They walked toward the house and veered toward the barn. "This is where you were, uh, born," Landon said. "Grandpa Karl made you here." He marched on in a daze, wondering if Holly and Bridget had made it back, as well. He glanced back at the cornfield. He hadn't thought of checking for their boats. There was no sign of the leaf-boats—or of the girls—from here.

Or of Max and his boat for that matter.

They reached the barn, and Landon led Jalopy inside. This was so strange. What else was he supposed to do? They went past the old car, JALOPY on its plate. And then into the lofty barn. The trapdoor was closed and covered with hay, as if it wasn't there. The scaffold had been dismantled, the poles and boards piled in a corner. All they needed was a stall for a horse. Landon looked around for a rope, but then realized Jalopy had no harness to fasten it to. Maybe he should leave her outside. No. He had to show Holly and Bridget. And Grandpa Karl. Maybe he would know what to do.

A commotion sounded outside. Distant cries. And a siren? Landon had never heard a siren wail in Button Up.

"I'll be back in a bit, okay, Jalopy? Just stay here and eat some hay or something." Feeling slightly guilty about locking her up, Landon gently closed the door, watching her. She merely stood looking into the barn.

Landon ran outside. More cries came from the other side of the house. He ran around to the front, where on the porch stood Grandpa Karl and Grandma Alice gazing toward town. Smoke rose from beyond the copse of trees at the top of the hill where the road went down. At the bottom of that hill was the Button Up Library.

"Oh, no."

People were on the road, striding or jogging toward town. The siren dropped in pitch, whirring softer.

"What happened?" Landon asked.

Grandma Alice turned, her hand on her breast. "Oh! Landon. Thank goodness you're okay. We were starting to worry!" Her eyes flicked back and forth. "Where are your sisters?"

Landon stared, speechless, before his grandfather touched Grandma Alice's arm and directed her, pointing toward the cornfield. "There they are."

How had they gotten behind him?

Grandpa Karl looked at Landon, his eyes full of wonder and questions. But when he spoke again, his voice sounded gruff with sadness. "Bart's Reading Room caught on fire."

Landon gasped. "What? How?"

Grandpa Karl's eyes flicked a shade darker as Grandma Alice muttered, "It was that boy Max."

Landon felt dizzy. Max? *He's still riding the dragon of death,* Landon thought sadly. He was too stunned to feel angry. Would that boy ever turn from evil?

"How do you know it was him?" Landon asked.

Grandpa Karl sighed. "Sheriff called me—twice. He was first on the scene at the fire. Then he called again when they apprehended the arsonist. Max. They've got him at the courthouse now. Behind bars."

"He's in jail?"

Grandma Alice folded her arms and declared, "Where he should be."

Landon looked at the smoke, for a moment picturing Volucer Ignis swooping from the sky to light the library on fire. "There wasn't anything else. . .spotted, was there?"

Grandpa Karl studied him, although his thoughts seemed to be someplace else. "Any. . .*thing?*" He looked concerned.

Landon shrugged. "I don't know. And the rest of the library?"

Grandpa Karl's eyes focused clearly. He sighed. "It's all right. They caught the fire in time to isolate it in the Reading Room."

Holly and Bridget were running over, holding hands. "There's smoke!" Bridget squealed. "What happened?"

Grandma Alice hugged the girls, and they all seemed to

soften. The fire was explained again, and Max's being in jail. Holly and Bridget looked at Landon, and he squinted. "Nothing else was spotted," he said, in case they were wondering about the dragon.

Landon started to feel restless, as if he should do something. Two thoughts occurred to him. The first was a question.

"Why did the sheriff contact you, Grandpa?"

Grandpa Karl cleared his throat. Putting his arm around Landon, he guided him to the door. "I have something to show you," he said.

Grandfather and grandson headed to the study. Landon thought he caught a faint whiff of smoke, as if someone had lit a match in the room and just snuffed it out. Then Landon thought of the tunnel behind the bookcase leading to Bart's Reading Room. The tunnel itself was probably hazy with smoke. It was all so sad and terrible.

Grandpa Karl opened a drawer in his desk and removed a small sheaf of papers. "This was only one sheet years ago, when it was first drawn up. Things get so complex with legalities and clauses these days." He held the papers to his chest, gazing deeply at Landon until Landon started feeling self-conscious.

"What?" Landon said.

Grandpa Karl smiled. His eyes traveled to the bookcase and then slowly back to Landon. "It may not seem like a good day to do this, but it's the right day. I know it is. And I've been looking forward to this for a long time."

Landon felt his heart beginning to pound, though he wasn't sure why. He glanced from his grandfather to the Bible on the desk. Beside the ancient book rested the stone with the word *dream* etched across it.

Handing the papers to Landon, Grandpa Karl said, "This is the deed to the Button Up Library and to this house. You've noticed, of course, that the two kind of go together."

Landon nodded, his heart racing. "The bookcase."

Grandpa Karl's smile grew. "I look forward to hearing all about your adventures, Landon. Yours and the girls'. We'll have some good stories to swap."

Landon was touching the papers, not sure if he'd heard his grandfather correctly. "These are for the library? And the house?"

Grandpa Karl let the papers go. "Yup. Been in this family for generations. All the way back to your great-great-great-great-grandfather—"

"Humphrey," Landon said.

Grandpa Karl's eyes glimmered. "Humphrey. That's right. Now I'm still listed in there"—he indicated the papers—"because you're not eighteen yet. But it's all spelled out that if anything should happen to me, the properties will remain in trust under your father's care until you turn eighteen. Then they'll belong to you."

"I don't know what to say. Or what to think, even."

"But you know who to turn to for guidance," Grandpa Karl said. "You understand what trust is."

"Grandpa?"

"Yes, Landon?"

"There is something I want to tell you."

Grandpa Karl put his hands on Landon's shoulders. "Yes? I'm all ears."

"Jalopy's back," Landon said. "I mean, Jalopy Two. She's in the barn."

Grandpa Karl's eyebrows shot up. "Really." He gave Landon's shoulders a gentle squeeze.

"Really," said Landon, smiling.

Seeing his Bible again on the desk, Landon realized what he needed to do. He knew why he'd felt restless on the porch. "Can I leave these here?" He lifted the papers and then set them on the desk.

Grandpa Karl's eyebrows were still perched high. "Sure. By all means. She's *in the barn*, you say?"

Picking up his Bible, Landon glanced back as he stepped out the door. "She is."

The only explanation he gave his grandmother and sisters as he raced by on the porch was, "I've got to go do something."

Carrying his Bible, he ran the length of the gravel driveway to the empty road, and then down the hill's winding path. The smoke had mostly cleared. A small crowd remained along the taped-off edge of the Button Up Library property. *That's my property,* Landon thought. The reality had yet to sink into his heart. He forced himself not to look at the charred, dripping corner where the Reading Room cabin had been. A few firefighters were examining the wreckage. Thankfully, the rest of the library stood as proudly and majestically as ever, the twin stone lions on guard out front.

Landon continued on down Main Street, crossing at the town's one blinking yellow light. He passed the bakery and the café and the barbershop, the hardware store, and a print shop.

When he reached the courthouse, he paused to catch his breath before proceeding inside.

There was no actual courtroom in the courthouse, but for some reason that's what everyone called it. Landon asked the deputy at the desk if he could see Max.

"You're that Snow boy, aren't you?" the deputy asked as he stood from behind the desk.

"That's right," said Landon. "My grandparents are Karl and Alice. They live up on—"

The deputy grinned, raising his hand. "Oh, I know. I know. Good people. So you want to see Max?" He shot Landon a questioning look, taking in the old book beneath his arm.

"Yes, please," said Landon. "I'd like to talk to him, if it's all right."

After studying him a moment longer, the deputy finally turned. "Come this way."

Landon followed him through a heavy, secure door and into a space along two jail cells. One was empty. In the other sat Max with his head in his hands. His hair and clothing were covered in soot.

"Take as long as you want," the deputy said to Landon. "He isn't going anywhere. Not today, anyway."

When the deputy had stepped out, Landon found a chair and pulled it up to the bars.

"Hey," he said. "You look like you did when I saw you in Bart's Reading Room in the fireplace. Are you always that filthy?"

"It's gone," Max said dully. "I burned it down." He glanced up only briefly. He didn't look or sound happy or proud or smug. He only looked and sounded. . .empty.

"I know," said Landon. He had to close his eyes, resisting the urge to become angry or hateful. He pictured the dragon and focused his anger toward him. Then he opened his eyes and saw his Bible. He pictured the man who had spoken to him from the Bible, and he felt peace.

"Do you know the last thing Bartholomew G. Benneford heard before he died?"

Max didn't move.

"He heard the book of John. A nurse read it to him in the hospital." Landon opened the Bible to John, cleared his throat, and began to read.

" 'In the beginning was the Word, and the Word was with God, and the Word was God. The same was in the beginning with God.' "

Landon continued reading, only stopping to get a drink of water (he had just read about "living water" in the fourth chapter), and to use the restroom a few chapters after that. Over an hour later, Landon reached the final verse, John 21:25: " 'And there are also many other things which Jesus did, the which, if they should be written every one, I suppose that even the world itself could not contain the books that should be written. Amen.' "

Landon looked up. Max hadn't stirred the entire time. He merely sat with his head between his hands.

"Do you know what Bartholomew G. Benneford said after hearing that?" Landon asked.

Very slowly, Max shook his head.

"He said, 'That's a lot of books.' " Landon made his voice gruff and tight, which was easy after reading aloud for over an hour. "Those were his final words. And then Bart died a happy man."

Landon closed his Bible, got up from his chair, and looked at his neighbor. *I forgive you,* he thought with a sigh. He left the courthouse.

The Button Up Library grounds were empty. The place was dark, closed up. As Landon crossed the street, passing the library steps, he thought about changing the name back to the original: Bartholomew G. Benneford's House of Knowledge and Adventure. Or how about *Landon Snow's* House of Knowledge and Adventure? Landon smiled to himself before settling on *The Button Up House of Knowledge and Adventure*. Yes, that had a nice clip to it.

When he reached the top of the hill, he slowed his steps, then stopped. It wasn't quite dark, although it had reached that long part of the summer day when the sun didn't want to let go and nighttime seemed content to put off its arrival. Silhouetted against the reddish sky was the figure of a horse.

"Jalopy?" Landon called to it. "How did you get out?"

No one else was around, and something told Landon it wasn't Jalopy. He moved closer, and the horse took a few tentative steps his way. Before this day, Landon hadn't seen any horses in Button Up. Had this one come from somewhere else? What was it doing on this road? How did it get here?

Something about it felt very familiar. But Landon wouldn't allow himself the thought until he was standing before the dark brown horse nose to muzzle. The horse's deep, shiny eyes knew Landon. And Landon knew him, too.

"Melech?"

Melech neighed and then said, "It is good to see you again, young Landon."

There was just enough light for a good ride along the cornfield and down to Lake Button Hole. When they came back, Landon dismounted and picked up his Bible, which he had set at the corner of his grandparents' driveway. It was too dark to read, so he stuck his finger between the pages where it had mysteriously opened to during his ride. When they reached the porch light, Landon opened the Bible and read these underlined words in Luke 17:21: "The kingdom of God is within you."

About the Author

R. K. Mortenson, an ordained minister in the Church of the Lutheran Brethren, has been writing poems and stories since he was a kid. A former Navy chaplain, Mortenson is a pastor in North Dakota. He serves a church in Mayville, where he lives with his wife, daughter, and two sons.